Talks to a Picture of Jesus

Gayla Morris

Talks To A Picture Of Jesus
Copyright © 2018
Gayla Morris
All rights reserved
Lyrics quoted are used by permission

Ordering: TPJ.Ordering.Info@gmail.com

Dedicated to my best friend, Lisa, my mom, who is a true Proverbs 31 woman, and to Hank, my benefactor and my Isaiah 46:11 man.

Table of Contents

1. Don't Ask a Woman Her Weight (But It's Okay to Ask a Guy) 7

2. Jammin' on the Jefferson and Mischievous Gordo 17

3. A Beautiful Wedding Dress and a Rat on a Rampage 29

4. Talks to a Picture of Jesus 57

5. Girls' Day Out and Guy's Day Busted 69

6. Get a Tissue and Laugh a Little 89

7. The God-incidence 113

8. The Big Day 129

Chapter 1

Don't Ask a Woman Her Weight (But It's Okay to Ask a Guy)

Let's start with Josie. Ladies first, right? The only child of Joy and Joseph Montgomery, Josie was a fun-loving, smart, pretty, and well-rounded young lady. Not well-rounded as in "well-rounded." Okay, maybe a little bit "rounded" but not a lot. Let's say well-adjusted. She was a normal, all-American woman pushing thirty. At least, that's what she likes to say. She's actually thirty-two, but that's neither here nor there.

She's a little hard to describe, ethnically, and usually checks the "Other" box on forms asking about race. Her dad is a war baby, from a black soldier and a Korean mother, and her mom is half Caucasian and half Latino, specifically Argentinian. Thus, Josie is just at home with calypso as she is with Kimchi. The mixture of races does make her hard to define, and she finds trying to explain her ethnicity to strangers rather fun. Sometimes she answers Sumerian out of playfulness, and most people have no clue that she's referring to a very ancient race, which could be the earliest known civilization that

Chapter 1

existed before the genetic dispersion. Every now and then, someone who is really into history catches her on that and they have a good laugh.

One thing really does set Josie apart from the crowd, however, even more so than her ethnicity. She loves Jesus with all her heart, and she really walks the walk. Thanks to Joy and Joseph, Josie grew up in a Christian home and had a solid, godly education. However, Josie was as normal a kid as they come and did her share of rebelling. It wasn't until her late teenage years that she decided to toe the line and be a Jesus-girl in earnest. Josie saw firsthand what living for yourself instead of the Lord could do to someone, and it really affected her deeply.

Three of Josie's friends made some imperfect choices. One of the girls she grew up with found herself in the family way, and instead of the embarrassment of telling anyone, she chose to go to a clinic and take care of it. Well, it didn't go over very well for her emotionally. No one knew what she had done, and probably no one would have ever known if the guilt of aborting her baby had not been too great a burden to bear, and ended up in a clinic of a different sort, where they help you mentally. Next, Josie's friend from band class was having a hard time keeping up with her schedule, and was taking meth to give herself that extra boost. Wow, what a mess she turned into. Sadly, she overdosed

Talks To A Picture Of Jesus

in Josie's senior year. Finally, one of the cheerleaders took her own life a few weeks before graduation. That shocked and rocked the entire community. Not a single person knew, until it came out in her note, that she was struggling with deep, dark depression, and suffered from very poor self-esteem and body image. Everyone thought she really had it all together and would turn into a fine, albeit driven, young lady.

Josie did the only thing she could think to do and got down on her knees and took all her cares, concerns, and tears to the Lord. That was the turning point for her.

That Fall, Josie went off to college and majored in Artistic Design, with a minor in Math. Weird, huh? She had a gift for mixing and matching fabrics and textiles and coming up with the most interesting and unique conceptions, and math actually helped her in her field. Who knew? She could sew the most fabulous creations without a pattern, and recover a thrift store dining room chair that you would swear came from a high end furniture store.

She and her mom were now co-owners of a boutique in a popular strip mall where Josie handled all the creative aspects and Joy managed the business end. It was working out well for them to work together, and Josie was very glad her mother didn't "mother" her during working hours. Joy had

Chapter 1

decided when they first discussed the possibility of a boutique and pooling their resources, that she would respect Josie's independence and not make her feel like a child at her own company. Josie was a full-rights partner and deserved to be treated as such. That's not to say Joy didn't let the occasional "are you sure you want to eat that?" slip out. But during her morning prayer time, she consistently asked the Lord to help her have a good working relationship with her daughter and that they would both seek Him first above all else. She was incredibly proud of not only her daughter's accomplishments, but also her unwavering walk with Jesus.

During college, Josie had one teacher in particular who did not care for her modest apparel. This teacher constantly marked down Josie's work with criticism such as "not enough cleavage," or "make the slit higher up on the thigh," etc. This went on all semester long, and when Josie finally told him she herself would not be comfortable wearing a gown with a slit that high, and that she was designing clothes for regular God-fearing people, he laughed at her and said, "You'll never amount to anything in this business. You might as well just drop out now." The sting of his words had her calling her mother that night, venting and crying, crying and venting.

For the first time, it dawned on Joy what Josie was giving up in order to follow Jesus. Joy had

Talks To A Picture Of Jesus

married right out of high school and hadn't faced some of the obstacles Josie was facing. That night Josie also told Joy about some of the guys she had dated in college, thinking they were good Christian guys and finding out the hard way that they were creeps and posers. Josie feared she would never get married because no one measured up. Joy was so torn between telling Josie to lighten up and live a little or stand her ground, even if it meant not getting married. Joy's heart broke for Josie, and she frequently asked God to supply Josie's need for marriage and family, but here they were ten years later and a handful of dates had not materialized into anything substantial.

Joy wondered if Josie was just being too picky, but after meeting a couple of the guys Josie met on a Christian dating site, she began to agree with her daughter. Where were all the godly young men? Nevertheless, Joy was grateful for all that the Lord had done for her daughter, and set her mind to praying for only God's best for her, nothing less.

Now let's meet Paul. Paul Hilliard is an all-around man's man. Need someone on your

Chapter 1

basketball team? You'll want to call Paul. Is your lawnmower broken? Paul has a knack for fixing anything from lawnmowers to computers and a lot of things in between. Do you need a new advertising campaign for your business? You'll definitely want to call Paul, that's his specialty. He likes that saying, "Jack of all trades, master of none," but he's got a pretty good handle on advertising, with a few promotions under his belt to prove it.

At 35, he is a vice president with Norris and Tuney, and a few hints have been dropped about his becoming a partner someday. Norris, Tuney and Hilliard – he likes the sound of that, and he's very grateful that God has given him this opportunity to work under Ken Norris and Lawrence Tuney, and that they have mentored him these past 15 years.

Paul started out in the mail room at 20, not expecting anything more than to fill his time and earn a little money during the summer months, then quitting as soon as school started back up. But Ken and Larry saw his good work ethic and convinced him to stay on part time while Paul earned his degree in Accounting. He never once saw himself as a marketer, he always thought his mild manner was actually more suited to accounting, but through Ken and Larry's mentorship, he came to realize and appreciate that marketing is not necessarily only about selling, it's also about meeting needs. When he finally learned to relax and focus on identifying

Talks To A Picture Of Jesus

and meeting needs instead of selling product, his campaign ideas began to flourish.

And speaking of meeting needs, there's one more thing Paul is really good at. Are you a little apprehensive about an upcoming surgery and need someone to pray for you? Paul is your man. Is your kid at home sick and you're stuck at work worrying about her? Do you need someone to pray for her? Paul will stop whatever he's doing and pray right then and there at your side. Is your marriage in trouble? He won't just pray for you once right then, he'll put you on his prayer list and pray for you every day. That's the kind of man he is, and those who know him well love this about Paul, even if they don't fully understand it.

Isn't prayer just something priests and pastors do? Or something rote that you say at mealtimes? Paul talked to God like He was there in the room with them, and it was fascinating that it was as if they were friends, rather than some distant all-powerful Being high up in the sky. A few of Paul's co-workers had even begun to pray like that just from simply following Paul's example. Yes ladies and gentlemen, Paul was a prayer warrior, among all the other things he was good at.

Now let's get to his stats, because men like stats, don't they? You can ask them how much they weigh and they won't even hesitate to answer because it's just a stat to them. But if you ask a

Chapter 1

woman her weight, whoa, you're taking your life in your hands! But Paul doesn't mind, he's six feet tall and weighs 210 lbs. He works out at the gym a few times a week, so he's muscly without being overly muscular, if you know the difference. Single, never married, two brothers and a sister, nine nieces and nephews out of the sister and one brother.

He thought he would be married by now, and would have contributed at least four more grandkids to his mom and dad's haul, but life threw him a curve ball when his girlfriend died in a terrible accident on the interstate ten years ago. Paul floundered for a few years after that, and almost decided to turn his back on God. He wasn't actually even a Christian at that point, but he didn't consider himself an atheist either. He was just a normal guy living a normal life and then boom! The rug was pulled out from under him.

He instinctively knew that God was the one to turn to, and yet God was the one he wanted to turn away from. How could a loving God allow the tragedy that goes on in this world? It's a valid question, one that millions just like Paul have asked. It's funny how God gets the blame whenever something bad happens in this fallen world instead of laying the blame where it belongs – our sin nature and the fact that we have the ability to choose sin over God. But this isn't a theological discussion at

Talks To A Picture Of Jesus

the moment, this is a story about divine intervention.

In His wisdom, God did not intervene the day Paul's girlfriend was killed. Instead, God sent a messenger to Paul in the form of one, Mark Troyer, a local pastor who led Paul to Christ and helped him discover all the reasons why he should turn to God instead of turning away from Him. To this day, Mark and Paul have remained steadfast friends. In addition to Sunday worship where Paul is a member of Mark's church, they also see each other on Tuesdays for men's basketball, every other Saturday for men's prayer breakfast, and not uncommonly sometimes out on the golf course or the batting cage whenever they feel the need for some "bro-time."

They've talked on occasion about Paul's marital status, or lack thereof, and prayed together only once that God would bring a godly young lady into Paul's life at the right time, however, only if it lined up with His will. Mark encouraged Paul by showing him the scripture that says anything we pray, if it is according to God's will, we can be sure we have it. So, they didn't fret and stew like girls quite often do when asking for a husband, and they didn't badger God with the same request over and over. No, they prayed about it together once and trusted that God would answer that prayer when the time was right. That was five years ago now. Paul

Chapter 1

secretly wondered if the time would ever be right, but he made up his mind to just ....trust.

Chapter 2

Jammin' on the Jefferson and Mischievous Gordo

"You are not my friend, and I want to punch you in the face right now!" Josie hurled this insult at the object of her disgust, and the object of her disgust ignored her and continued to beep, beep, beep until she got out of bed and turned it off. Walking back to the bed, she said, "I'm sorry clock, you didn't deserve that. You are my friend because you make sure I get up and get going instead of letting me sleep through important appointments and meetings."

It was a little tempting to get back in bed, because she'd had a late night sewing the sweetest little rosettes to her latest endeavor; however, her outburst at her clock and subsequent apology had her remembering she had an appointment this fine Tuesday morning with the young lady for whom the rosettes were intended. So instead, she got down on her knees at her bedside, as was her daily habit,

Chapter 2

and gave her first five or so minutes to God. She thanked Him for a good day, regardless of whether or not it actually was good, because even when our days are not good, God is still good. He's still sitting on His heavenly throne, watching over His followers, directing their steps, and causing their circumstances to work out ultimately for good, for those who love Him.

She prayed for her best friend Chloe, also a regular habit but maybe not a daily one. Sometimes her prayers focused on the same events, circumstances, or people. Other times a different friend would pop into her head for seemingly no reason, so she prayed for that person instead. Chloe got a lot of prayer time because she had not yet asked Jesus to save her, and as Josie's best friend, that weighed heavily on her heart.

Sometimes Josie stayed on her knees longer than five minutes, and other times her bladder would not let her. This morning, her bladder cooperated and Josie was able to lift several people up to the Lord in prayer. Linda, who was getting married in a couple of months, needed wisdom as a new wife to honor her husband and have a loving, long-lasting marriage. Benny, her intended, also needed wisdom to love Linda as Jesus loves us and be a faithful, godly husband. Josie's dad, Joseph, was having foot surgery in a few weeks, so she prayed that the procedure would go well and that

Talks To A Picture Of Jesus

her dad would heal quickly. A lady at church had had two miscarriages already, and had asked the entire church to shower her with prayers of protection and health for her baby. She had almost decided not to share that she was even pregnant because of the heartbreak of the miscarriages, but changed her mind after a message on a passage in James that talked about fervent and consistent prayer, that it was powerful and effective. Since that night was testimony night at the evening service, she did share her good news and asked everyone to blanket her with that kind of fervent and consistent prayer. Many in the congregation went ahead and got up right then and there to surround mother and baby, and lift them up to the Lord, and promised to be faithful about it. Josie was so glad to be a part of a loving church family like that.

"Alright Lord, I have to get up now, but I'll talk to you again at noon. Amen." And with that, Josie got up, turned on K-Love®[i], and started getting ready for the day that the Lord had made.

She stepped on the scale and grimaced. "Ugh!" She had just joined a gym and was hoping to get trim and toned in no time at all, but a week of workouts had her actually up a pound. The guy who signed her up warned her that this might happen as she started building muscle, and she thought at the time that it was just a sales pitch to keep people

Chapter 2

going to the gym and parting with their money, but now she hoped he was right.

She surveyed herself in the mirror, not completely in love with what she saw, but not thoroughly offended by it either. Like so many people these days, she could stand to lose a few pounds, but at least she was fairly well proportioned. There were things she liked about herself, like her wavy brown hair that only needed a curling iron here and there, and her cheekbones that hardly needed any blush. She considered those her best features, but she didn't even notice her wide-set dark brown eyes that could envelop you in comforting compassion or pierce you with a look that you knew meant business. She considered herself mildly attractive, but not runway material. However, she also knew that a good deal of attractiveness was confidence; so she made up her mind to try to portray confidence even when she didn't feel it.

Before long, she was spreading jelly on a piece of toast, then leaving her apartment to head down to her Ford Fiesta parked in her reserved spot. Once inside, she ran through her preset Christian radio stations, K-Love®, Air1®, AFR®[ii], and FLR®[iii] looking for something to jam to on her way to work. She had a low dance threshold. That means when a good song comes on, Josie could not help bobbing her head, tapping her feet, waggling her arms, or

Talks To A Picture Of Jesus

any other sort of movement set to a catchy beat. Sitting still during a good song was almost akin to torture! Lol, not really, but Josie liked to tell her mom and dad that was why she could not sit still at church as a kid. Even when they weren't singing, music was still running through her head. She could get away with that with her dad, since she had inherited his low dance threshold, but her mom was a different story.

Those with a high dance threshold could remain motionless, and that was their prerogative. She, on the other hand, liked to express herself, so it was no big surprise that when she pulled up to a red light at the Jefferson Parkway, a very busy six-lane road, she was jamming to one of her favorite Toby Mac songs, singing about when love broke through.

Since she was first in line at the light, she noticed a Ford Explorer a few lanes over, across the intersection, headed in the opposite direction. At first she only admired the SUV. She had been considering trading in her Fiesta for the more spacious Explorer and whenever she saw them, she took note of the different year's body styles and colors in order to start looking online to get a feel for prices. This was a really nice silver one, probably a little newer than she could afford, but a girl can dream, can't she?

Seconds later, she noticed that the guy in the Explorer was grooving along to the same beat

Chapter 2

Josie was, beat per beat, in sync. She wondered if he were listening to the same Toby Mac song, and thought, "How cool is that!" The light turned green for those in the turning lane, and she continued to watch as the music changed to a very sweet Francesca Battistelli song inviting God to write His story on her heart. She noticed that their heads kept the same beat, and she sort of hoped that he would look her way, but he continued to stare straight ahead while his head bobbed.

Soon the light turned green for all the North-South traffic, and she was whizzing through the intersection, passing her gym on the left and heading towards Jay Jay's, the boutique she and her mom ran together. The man in the Explorer was replaced with visions of lace and rosettes as she began to mentally prepare for today's fitting, hoping Linda would be pleased with the progress, and that she would finally have the shoes she planned to wear, so Josie could begin working on the hem and train detail.

Paul glanced at the clock in the dashboard of his SUV as he pulled out of the gym parking lot, pleased with his morning workout. It was 7:10 a.m.

Talks To A Picture Of Jesus

and, as usual, he would get to work between 7:20 and 7:30, a good half hour before the official start time of 8:00 a.m. He wasn't a brown-noser, so getting there early had nothing to do with getting ahead and/or earning points with the bosses; he just liked the early morning quiet when he could spend a little time in preparation, and also prayer and meditation before the daily grind began. The verse of the day was announced and recited on the radio and he was pleasantly surprised that it was Philippians 1:6. Just last night, a light bulb had turned on inside his head about its meaning.

A few years ago, he would have called it a coincidence that the verse was being repeated this morning, but now lately he calls them God-incidences, when God has specifically orchestrated something, be it as simple as a repeated Bible verse or as complicated as something highly detailed that He had planned before the foundation of the world.

Philippians 1:6 had been the focal point of the daily devotional he read last night, just before going to bed; so, to hear it again this morning seemed to be a God-incidence. It meant God wanted him to sit up and pay attention. In particular, the part that said that the good work which God had begun in us will continue until the day of Jesus Christ was just a tiny bit puzzling, not enough for him to ask his best friend and pastor, Mark, whom he considered to be a very wise man of

Chapter 2

God, but enough for him to say recently and a little tiny bit flippantly, "Holy Spirit, if you wouldn't mind clearing that up for me in my head, that would be great."

He could understand that the good work God had begun in him would continue until his death, that made sense. But for it to continue until the day of Jesus Christ? Too many people had died since the writing of the Apostle Paul until now, and will continue to pass away until the day Jesus actually returns.

But last night as he reread that verse for about the hundredth time since the many years ago that he was saved, the idea of a family tree popped into his head. He didn't know why at first, but he kept pondering it and thinking about it in connection to Philippians 1:6, and then finally it hit him. Whatever we do to advance the kingdom of Heaven doesn't end when we die, it continues on in the next person until they pass away, and then the next person after that.

He thought of the verse in Ephesians 1 about God working everything according to His plan and how, like a family tree, it branches out, spreads, branches out some more and weaves patterns throughout time and history that we can just barely comprehend from our perspective, but that forms a beautiful tapestry from God's perspective. Then when the verse was repeated again this morning, he

Talks To A Picture Of Jesus

said, "Lord, thank you so much for considering me teachable!" One of his favorite Toby Mac songs came on over the radio after that, and he didn't even realize that his head was bobbing, because he was still focused on the good work God had begun in him, and wondered what plans God might have for him, and who it might live on in.

When he pulled into the parking lot of Norris and Tuney at 7:27 a.m., his thoughts turned to Jordan Tuney, Larry's nephew. He wondered what mischief "Gordo" would be up to today and hoped he had the grace to handle it. Jordan had been born Gordon, after his grandfather, but felt that name was not befitting his suave style and smooth moves, so he had it legally changed to Jordan when he was old enough to do it without parental consent. He made it clear to his uncle that he would not answer to Gordon, and for the most part, Larry obliged him. But every now and then, Larry would accidentally on purpose call him Gordo.

One time it was during a heated argument and Jordan, who had a serious temper, nearly decked his uncle. But Paul, who saw it coming, broke Jordan's stance by coming up behind him and pushing in the back of Jordan's knee with his foot just as Jordan was about to swing, causing Jordan to go down hard on one knee. Larry yelled at him, "This is my company, Gordo, and you'll not only do as I say, but you'll answer to Mary Margaret if I tell

Chapter 2

you to! If you don't like it, there's the door, don't let it hit you in the butt on the way out!"

Jordan had had it out for Paul since then, smack-talking him whenever possible. As passive-aggressively as he could, without being outright aggressive, Jordan would denigrate Paul's campaign ads, calling them old-school, or fine for the uneducated, all the while with a smile on his face and a seemingly positive attitude. Then he would put forth his own ideas which usually involved sex and/or scantily clad women.

That was Jordan, a hot-tempered know-it-all, rude dude and booze hound. Larry wished he hadn't promised his sister-in-law that he would give Jordan a job after he had been expelled from college and fired from three previous employers, but in honor of his brother, who had died in Afghanistan before Jordan was even born, Larry had tried his best to be there for Nancy and the baby. Nancy had gone on to remarry three different times, but each one ended in divorce. Larry suspected Nancy had married each time for money, and each time the money ran out, so did the relationship.

That left Jordan with a plethora of so-called fathers, none of which loved him unconditionally. Paul wanted to show Jordan the love of God, but quite often the best he could do was just hold his tongue. This morning, in light of his new understanding of Philippians 1:6, he thanked God for

Talks To A Picture Of Jesus

continuing whatever work He had begun involving himself and Jordan, and asked for wisdom to deal with whatever Jordan does next.

Chapter 3

A Beautiful Wedding Dress and a Rat on a Rampage

Josie was knee-deep in satin, lace, and organza when Joy came in about half an hour after her daughter. "Agent Jay," Josie said in her driest voice, with a curt nod.

"Agent Jay," Joy good-naturedly replied. Josie was a bit of a character, and had Joy often laughing and shaking her head. She was just like Joseph, Joy thought. Both had such a quirky sense of humor.

Before the store became a reality and they were discussing business names, Josie and Joseph had joked around about it being a cover for the Men in Black, with aliens hiding amongst the goods. Since all three of them were Agent Jays, it made perfect sense to Joseph and Josie to name the store Agent Jay's. Joy's good sense prevailed in the end, and the store name became Jay Jay's.

Still, if Josie was the first one to arrive, sometimes she would clasp her hands with her forefingers pointed up, and say to the empty room,

Chapter 3

"Alright you alien scum, prepare to be disintegrated!" Then, "Pew, pew, pew," as she shot at the aliens pretending to be mannequins, pillows, monkey-laden lamps, or any of the sundries that might grace the shop with their presence that week.

Her quirky sense of humor really did lead her to buy a monkey-laden lamp at a garage sale, complete with a rotating inner carousel, and adorned with a dancing elephant on top. "Oh Josie, for crying out loud, what on Earth are you going to do with that?" her mother demanded to know.

"You'll see, mom. It'll be fabulous!" And it was, after Josie cleaned it up, repainted it, added a lot of bling in the form of beads and jewels, with a little ribbon-wrapped tulle draped around it. It sold that very day, when Josie displayed it on a mirrored pillar swathed with iridescent lamé, in a place of honor in the center of the store. Your eyes couldn't help but be drawn to it as soon as you entered, so before the day's end, her garage sale bargain had added a nice little profit to the coffers that her mother could not deny was nothing short of brilliance.

"Ooooo, Linda's dress is really coming along!" Joy leaned down to inspect the fanning splay of rosettes that came over one shoulder, down the bodice, wrapped around the waist and merged with the organza that came over the other shoulder, then down the back to form the train.

Talks To A Picture Of Jesus

This was the first and possibly only wedding dress Josie had ever designed and sewed for a customer. Her designs were usually gowns and formals intended for quinceañeras, proms, and other special events for which she became known among the Christian community – beautiful creations that didn't compromise with plunging necklines and the thigh-high slits found at bridal shops and department stores. Normally she kept a selection of several dresses in various sizes and fabrics on a rack in the shop, but quite often someone would come in asking for a special order, and if she felt she could accommodate it, she would accept the order.

It started with the moms at her church who needed prom dresses for their daughters and didn't want them exposed to anyone and everyone with bulging eyes and wagging tongues. At first their daughters balked at the thought of homemade dresses, especially ones that did not follow the current Katy Perry, Taylor Swift, and Beyoncé fashion trends, but when they saw how unique her designs were, and that they could not only look completely fabulous, but boast about having a one-of-a-kind formal, word spread throughout their youth group and then to their friends at school. It became fashionable to have a "Josie M." original.

"Wow, has this been challenging!" Josie replied to her mother's compliment.

Chapter 3

"Yes, but you're earning five months of income in what, two months?"

"I'm not sure it's worth it, mom. I think I'd rather stick to formals for the foreseeable future."

"That's fine honey, but remember, you're doing this as unto the Lord, and He has blessed you tremendously for it. He's given you the talent and creativity. He has provided for you every step of the way, and you have honored Him with hard work and uncompromised standards. It's a pretty good partnership, and now He's blessing you monetarily." Then with a little bit of slyness in her voice, Joy added, "And pretty soon, who knows? You might be blessed to be able to design and sew your own wedding dress, and with the money you've earned, think of the magical wedding! Oh, the flowers, the candles, the arched trellis...."

Before she could get too far into the wonderful details of this, as of yet, nonexistent wedding, Josie stopped her with, "Hold on a minute, Mother-of-the-Bride. If you think you're getting out of your motherly duty of paying for my wedding just because I'm rolling in the dough, you'd better think again!"

"I would never do that, Dear! Your father and I can't wait to pawn you off on some unsuspecting yokel, who has no idea what a firecracker you are!" They both laughed good-naturedly, and Joy kissed her daughter's forehead.

Talks To A Picture Of Jesus

Josie added a little wryly, "Yeah right, as if."

Joy recognized the yearning in her daughter's tone of voice, and said, "It will happen honey, in God's perfect timing." Josie's face flashed hope, discouragement, longing, and faith all seemingly at once before responding,

"I know, mama. I don't want anything less than His best for me, so I'll wait. And wait, and wait, and wait."

"I know you will, baby," Joy said, brushing back a lock of hair that had fallen across one eye. "And remember, that verse also says 'Be of good courage' while you wait. Take strength in that," referring to Psalm 27:14.

Linda and her mom, Ernestina, showed up promptly at 10:00 a.m. for the fitting, and were both ecstatic about the wedding dress. Josie and the two ladies were in the back room of the shop, which served as the stockroom, the breakroom, the office, and the dressing room. Ernestina exclaimed, "Oh my goodness, Josie! I can't believe you designed this! Holy cow, I've never seen anything like it!"

Linda was an absolute vision standing before them, sheathed in white, her dark, curly hair pulled up in loose ringlets, with tendrils on either side pulled out to spiral in the most becoming fashion around her small, heart-shaped face. Her olive skin looked healthy and glowing against the white of the

Chapter 3

dress, and Josie suspected she was wearing shimmering body lotion.

Joy, who was watching the store while Josie was attending to Linda, managed to steal away for a minute for a sneak peek at Linda in her wedding gown, and was blown away by what Josie had managed to pull off. Linda was a pretty girl, but at this moment, she took their breath away.

"Linda!" she said, "you are positively stunning!" Linda's already pink cheeks turned just a shade pinker as she turned first right, then left in the mirror, and replied,

"Thank you Mrs. Montgomery. Do you think Benny will like it?"

Linda's mom made a pffbt sound and said, "Honey, Benny would adore you in a potato sack. You don't need to worry about whether or not Benny will like it."

To which Joy added, "Trust me Linda, Benito won't be able to take his eyes off you!" Linda was smiling so much throughout the fitting that she told everyone she was starting to get a headache from it.

Thankfully she had finally settled on a pair of shoes, so Josie was able to pin up the hem at the right length. Linda's mom, Ernestina, had previously purchased a formal for her daughter while she was still in high school, and when Linda and Benito had announced their engagement shortly after

Talks To A Picture Of Jesus

graduation, Ernestina approached Josie about the possibility of making the wedding dress.

At first, Josie turned her down, saying it would take too long, be too much work, and cost an incredibly extravagant amount. Ernestina could not care less about the cost. Linda was their only daughter, and she and her husband, Hector, wanted to give her the fairytale wedding their own parents had not been able to afford in their youth. And Benito, whom they already loved and treated like a son, had joined the military and would be heading off to boot camp within six months of graduation, which is why they consented to the wedding, considering both of them were so young.

There were conditions, however, that they expected both Linda and Benito to abide by in exchange for this extravagant wedding. Linda had enrolled in community college and was expected to attend faithfully whether Benny was in town, at boot camp, or deployed, and Benny made a promise to take advantage of the educational benefits offered to all military personnel in exchange for their service to our country. The wedding was now a month away, and Benny would be heading off to boot camp two weeks after that. Josie prayed for them both whenever she thought about it, because what a way to start a marriage!

After that, Josie and Joy put in a good day's work, and had several customers stop in for a

Chapter 3

Tuesday. It always amazed them how many people stopped in throughout the week during working hours, and they wondered how those people could afford to be out shopping instead of out working.

Not that they were complaining. On the contrary, their boutique was quite dependent on those who could afford to be out shopping during the week. Their Saturday hours were abbreviated in order to give them a break, so only one of them had to be there a few hours, along with their young apprentice.

They had a part-time helper whose name was Sylvia. On weekdays, she worked from 5:00 p.m. until closing time at 8:00 p.m. and Saturdays from 9:00 a.m. until closing time at 3:00 p.m. The store was doing well enough that Joy was almost ready to broach the subject of another part-timer, in order for them to have Saturdays completely off. But for right now, Sylvia was a lifesaver in that Josie and Joy often needed to be in the backroom, inventorying goods, painting furniture, running the books, and all the other requirements and time stealers of operating a business.

Sylvia could be trusted to close up on her own, so frequently, Josie left at 5:00 p.m. in order to go to the gym before going home or to her parents' house for dinner.

Less frequently, she left at 5:00 in order to go out with friends. They might go to a movie, or

Talks To A Picture Of Jesus

even just out to a coffee shop for a good night of girl talk. It was a semblance of a personal life, but at least it was there. Most of her friends were now married with children, but a couple of the girls were now divorced, so every so often, they were able to arrange for a babysitter. One of the girls in her Bible study was still single, and of course, there was Chloe, but she lived three hours away now.

As if on cue, just before 5:00 p.m., Josie's phone began to sing to her, "You make me feel like dancing, I want to dance the night away…." Joy did not need the announcement as to whom it was, she knew that ring very well, but Josie still exclaimed, "It's Chloe!" Josie had only three personalized ring tones, Chloe, her mom, and her dad. Her mom's ringtone was Mama Mia, while her dad's was Josh Groban's You Raise Me Up.

"Chloe! I was just thinking about you!"

"Hey girlfriend! I know, I'm unforgettable, aren't I?"

"Ha!" Josie began to sing, "Unforgettable, that's what you are….. Unforgettable, though near or far….."

"Ha ha ha ha ha! Man, I miss you, Josie! So, guess what? I'm coming up there on Friday!"

"Shut up! Wooooo!"

"I know! Actually, it's a business trip, but I'm going to mix business with pleasure, baby! So, can I stay with you?"

Chapter 3

"Huh, a weekend business trip, that's kind of weird, isn't it?"

"I don't know, you've got to go where the clients are, play nice with their schedules, etcetera. It's no biggy."

"Yeah, I guess that's true. So, when are you meeting with this so-called Mr. Big Shot Client that you have to give up your weekend for? Not that I mind, I'm so jazzed you're coming up!"

"Friday night. It's sort of a cocktail mixer-type party. But I'll be there probably Friday around noon. So, can I stay with you?"

"Oh my gosh, Chloe! Do you even have to ask?" A few more minutes on the phone and it was all set. Sylvia had clocked in a little before Josie's cell phone rang, and she was available to work Friday afternoon, so Josie would be able to take that afternoon off to go gallivanting around town with Chloe.

There were a couple of red flags in that phone conversation that Josie did not want to dwell on, so she pushed them out of her mind. Business is business, and if she has to meet a client on a Friday night, so be it. She knew Chloe was a bit of a wild woman, but surely this would all be very professional, wouldn't it?

Talks To A Picture Of Jesus

Paul walked into the fifth floor offices of Norris and Tuney, and was pleased to see that the lights were on and the alarm was off. Even though he usually arrived by 7:30 a.m. or sooner, Victor was normally there anywhere from 7:00 to 7:15. The one morning Paul walked in and found the lights off and the alarm on, he immediately called the police and asked that they check on Victor at home.

Paul's instincts were right. Victor had had a heart attack, and even though it had not killed him, the resulting fall had incapacitated him. At 63, Victor was not quite ready to retire; however, it was generally understood that Victor would not be retiring at 65 either. He'd lost his wife, Grace, to lung cancer several years ago, and no one believed Victor would last long after retirement.

Thankfully, Ken and Larry were of a mind to let Victor work as long as he wanted. He worked in graphics and didn't care for a lot of the "new-fangled" technology they were using these days. He was an excellent sketch artist and preferred to put pencil to paper. Some of the other ad executives didn't care for his old fashioned ways, but Paul didn't mind, so he let Victor come up with the initial

Chapter 3

artwork on his ads, before sending the approved campaigns to the tech wizards.

Paul and Victor had developed a special comradery after the heart attack. Paul had gone to the hospital as soon as he was able to clear his schedule, in order to go pray with Victor. He had also stayed several hours because Victor wanted someone else to be there when the doctor came in to give the prognosis. They had not been close before; in fact, there was a little aloofness on Victor's part because Paul had joined the firm as a young "hotdog" and had quickly climbed the ladder. Victor knew that Paul's campaigns were good and deserved recognition, but there was just something about a young guy going from the mailroom to the Board room that made Victor want to bah humbug.

But all that changed the moment Paul walked into his hospital room. Victor had broken down and cried in Paul's presence; his brush with mortality had left him very fragile. Paul had gently spoken to him about making things right with God, and that Jesus' sacrifice on the cross had been payment for our sin. Paul told him about his own struggle after his girlfriend had died, and that he had finally found peace when he gave his life to Jesus, a peace that he didn't really even understand, but was there nonetheless.

Victor listened intently at first, but eventually he interrupted Paul and said, "I'm ready

Talks To A Picture Of Jesus

now. I want to give my life to Jesus, too. How do I do it?" For the second time, Victor cried like a baby in front of Paul, but this time they were tears of joy as a flood of forgiveness and faith washed over him. Victor had Paul to thank now for both his temporal life and his eternal one, because Paul had shared the Good News.

"That young hotdog left a half-eaten sandwich on his desk again last night, and a rat or a mouse or something found it." Those were the words Paul was greeted with that morning.

Paul was laughing as he replied, "Good morning to you too, Victor. I'll call building maintenance and have them bring up some rat and mouse traps."

"I brought a shovel in from my truck. I'm going to try to break its neck if I can." That struck Paul as amusing.

"Ha, ha, ha! You keep a shovel in your truck, huh? In case you need to bury the evidence?"

With a grin and a shrug, Victor replied, "You never know."

"So, you've got it under control then? No traps?"

Victor countered with, "Nah, go ahead and call them. With my luck, I'd aim for a mouse and end up cutting off someone's big toe. I'd feel badly about that, unless it were Jordan's."

41

Chapter 3

Paul asked matter-of-factly, "Hey, Victor, why did the mouse stay inside?"

"How should I know? Am I some sort of rat-whisperer?"

"Because it was raining cats and dogs." Paul could tell a joke without cracking a smile, so it wasn't until the punchline that you realized he had you going.

Victor laughed, "You're kind of a dork, you know that, right?" That didn't faze Paul at all.

"Why do mice need oiling?"

"I don't know, but I have a sinking feeling you're going to tell me."

"Because they squeak."

"Ha, ha, ha, ha, ha!"

"What squeaks as it solves crimes?"

"Oh my goodness, I'm afraid to ask."

"Miami mice!"

"Ha, ha, ha, ha, ha! Alright, that's enough out of you! This mouse ain't going to laugh it's head off. Let's get some mouse traps up here and watch all the women try to work standing on their chairs."

Paul was chuckling as he walked into his office and picked up the phone to call maintenance. It wasn't a coincidence that he had a few mouse jokes under his belt. He and Mark were constantly pulling bad jokes like that out of the blue on each other. The goal was to see who could last the longest without busting up first, and they were

Talks To A Picture Of Jesus

pretty evenly matched. They had so much fun with it that they decided to host a community outreach night at church with a bad-dad-jokes competition. Those who had signed up were even getting sponsors to raise money for their senior citizens' trip to Branson, Missouri.

The seniors formed this excursion every year. However, because so many of them were on pensions and social security, Mark didn't want anyone to miss out for lack of funds, so he organized a funds raiser every year to make sure anyone who wanted to go was able to go.

To get the community involved, the men of the church went around the neighborhood asking for sponsors, stressing that they had to come in order to keep them honest. It was a dollar for every joke they were able to withstand with a straight face, but most of the church members were sponsoring up to ten dollars a joke.

There were some men who they were sure would be out right off the bat, so they were also accepting flat donations. This was a first for their church and everyone was very excited about it. Most of all, Mark was excited about a new opportunity to share the Gospel with some who might not come to church otherwise.

After the call to building maintenance, Paul checked Jordan's cubicle and saw the evidence – the remnants of a sandwich that had been severely

Chapter 3

eaten by the lucky creature, along with mouse droppings.

Jordan could be so aggravating. When was he going to grow up, Paul wondered. "Lord, he's the kind of man You were talking about when You told us to pray for our enemies, and I honestly don't want to. I'm sorry about that, but You know my thoughts and there's no point in trying to hide it from You. But his biggest problem is not that he's a jerk, it's that he does not know You, and right now he doesn't even want to have anything to do with You. I need You to fill me with Your grace in order to be able to show him grace. I need You to constantly remind me that You've forgiven me so that I can remember to forgive him. I want him to see You in me. If nothing else, Lord, even though I can't stand the guy, please help him to see You in me. You are his only hope, and I humbly ask You to knock even louder on the door of Jordan's heart. Please be irresistible to him, and help me to do my part in Your kingdom work. Amen."

It was time to focus on work now, because Paul had a big presentation for a cereal company. Willow Grains had put word out that they were ending their contract with their existing marketing firm, and would be previewing ad campaigns from three competing firms, including Norris and Tuney. All of the ad execs had presented ideas to Ken and Larry, and they had decided to go with Paul's ideas.

Talks To A Picture Of Jesus

It would be a nice account to snag, and Paul was jazzed about it.

Jordan's submission was geared toward a young hip hop demographic, because he hadn't done his research on the Willow Grains mission statement and thought loud music and bling would sell. Paul tried to tell him that marketing was less about selling, and more about meeting needs, but it went in one ear and out the other.

Jordan was visibly miffed when Ken and Larry said they thought Paul's campaign had the best chance of success. Jordan seemed to think that as Larry's nephew, he was due special treatment, and when he didn't get it, he got angry and resentful. But anytime Larry had tried to give Jordan personal life-empowering advice, Jordan retorted with "You're not my father, so back off!" So, why Jordan thought Larry owed him anything was a mystery to everyone. Larry had been kind enough to give him a job and he should shut up and be grateful. That wasn't how Jordan saw it though. He had a very me-centric attitude.

People started arriving just before 8:00 a.m., and that's when the fun really began. Karen and Monique saw Victor poking around the cubicles with a shovel and started shrieking while jogging in place, arms flailing. Victor wasn't very reassuring when he said, "Calm down ladies. It's just a scared little

Chapter 3

mouse. The worst it can do is nibble on your toes, not kill you."

"VICTOR!" They collectively cried out. That sent them up on their chairs, and it was pretty good timing because the mouse darted out of one cubicle and ran cattycorner into another one. The ladies screamed, and Victor pounced.

That was the scene Larry walked in on. His look of bewilderment quickly turned to that of disgusted understanding, so he hollered out to Victor, who was now down at the other end of the large cubicle-filled great room.

"Was it Gordon again?" He always referred to Jordan as Gordon when we wasn't around, and saved Gordo for when he really wanted to jab at him.

"You betcha, boss, every week like clockwork."

Shaking his head, Larry headed for his office, but Monique added as he was walking, "That jerk could not care less that all that construction is going on in that field next door and driving the mice in. Larry, you need to whup that boy good," and added under her breath, "or I just might do it for you."

Mitch and Susie were next to enter the great room, but Susie shook her head and vehemently said, "No, no, no, no, no! Not today!" She turned right around and walked back out to reception, which was her station. She would have liked to put

Talks To A Picture Of Jesus

her lunch in the fridge in the kitchen, but she wasn't about to walk through that rat-infested room.

Mitch made his way to his cubicle, laughing at the girls and intentionally trying to startle them. Tall and lanky, Mitch was definitely the office clown. That's what made it so funny when he screamed like a girl and got up, not on a chair, but on his desk when the mouse scurried out from under it, running over Mitch's foot in its hurry to get to safety. "Oh my gosh! Oh my gosh! Oh my gosh! Victor, get it! Get it! Get it!"

Several people from the departments down the hall, who enter the offices through an employee entrance on the other side of the building, had come down the hall to see what the commotion was, and belly laughed at Mitch's outburst and Victor's subsequent battle with his make-shift weapon of a shovel.

And that was the scene Ken walked in on, with building maintenance right behind him. He was not amused. "Calm down everyone. Julio is here with traps. If you'll all please just go to your desks and offices, and stop this ruckus, Julio can get to work and catch this thing. This is a professional office, not a circus." He said it in a tone that meant business, and everyone knew better than to let even a peep out, so Mitch and the girls trepidatiously got down and looked around for the mouse before sitting down.

Chapter 3

Paul had been standing there the whole time, watching the histrionics, since his office bordered the great room. Larry's executive office was two doors down from his, and Ken's corner office was another door down from Larry's. Ken did not go right to his office though, he stopped at Larry's.

"Larry," Ken started out, but Larry knew what was coming, so he jumped in with, "I know, I know, Ken. The kid's got to go," he admitted.

Ken replied, "You've done all you could for him, he just doesn't want anybody's help. Heck, he doesn't even know he needs help."

"Yeah, I know. But to be fair, we're still going to have a mice problem for as long as that construction is going on next door. He just won't be adding to it by leaving food all over the place. Man, I'm almost glad his dad isn't around to see what a spoiled little twerp his son is. But then again, if he had survived Afghanistan, maybe Gordon would have turned out differently."

Ken huffed, "Cut the bull, Larry, you know that ten percent of who we are is what happens to us and the other ninety percent is how we respond to it."

"Preaching to the choir, man, preaching to the choir. Listen, do me a favor, will you? This is Tuesday. Let's at least let the kid work through the

Talks To A Picture Of Jesus

rest of the week so he gets a full paycheck, and I'll let him go on Friday."

Ken agreed and said, "Alright, but I'm holding you to it, Larry. He's been enough of a disturbance already. Friday it is."

It only took about fifteen minutes until there was a loud SNAP! and there was a collective gasp heard coming from the cubicles. Seven of the cubicles were occupied by that time, but the offending cubicle was as of yet unoccupied. Monique was heard loudly whispering, "Get Julio up here! Somebody get that monster out of here, pronto!" But just then, Jordan walked in from reception. As usual, he acted like he owned the place, with a smug smile and peacock sort of gait. He had already heard about the commotion from Susie in reception and thought it was hysterically funny.

"Morning plebeians! So you liked my little present, huh?"

Monique tended to be outspoken, so she was the first to respond with, "You're such a jerk, Jordan! You'd better wipe that smile off your face or I'll do it for you!"

"Monique, you can't even wipe your nose. Why don't you just sit your butt back down before I smack it! This wouldn't have happened if I'd had an office like I deserve!"

Chapter 3

That's when everyone joined in with, "In your dreams!" and "You deserve an office like a pig deserves a castle!" and "You think a mouse can't find food in an office as well as a cubicle? What a moron!"

Paul heard all this from his office but did not join in. Yes, Jordan was a jerk. But Paul also knew that hurt people hurt people. He didn't understand that phrase when he first heard it, but Mark explained it like this in a sermon a long time ago, "People who are hurting or have been hurt by someone at some point in their life, tend to lash out at other people, and I've come to understand that it's part of our sin-nature. Hurt people, adjective-noun, hurt people, verb-noun. But forgiveness is God-natured and He empowers us to look beyond the hurt that we are receiving and see the hurt in the one giving it. And folks, it's a powerful thing to be able to forgive. It takes a lot more strength to forgive than to lash back, but it frees you from the chains and bonds of bitterness, resentfulness, malice, you name it, all that ugly stuff. When you let it go, you're not carrying that weight of bondage anymore. You can drop it off at the cross and be free from it."

Paul wished there were something he could do or say to help Jordan understand that he could be free from this self-imposed bondage, but Jordan was not receptive to it. Paul had that Willow Grains

Talks To A Picture Of Jesus

presentation today anyway, so he had to put Jordan out of his mind for the time being and make sure he was ready with the pitch.

After about an hour and a half of reviewing and reciting, he got up to go to the men's room. When he walked in, he saw Jordan cleaning up something off the counter, sniffing and wiping his nose. Paul's heart sank. It was a worst-case scenario.

"Does Larry know you're doing that?"

"Shut up, mama's boy. I guarantee you, you and I are going to meet in a dark alley someday, and I'm going to lay a whupping on you that puts you in the hospital."

Jordan intentionally got in Paul's face, thinking Paul would flinch and back away, but Paul stood his ground and with a steely voice replied, "You can try, but you won't succeed. Jordan, you're wasting your life. Your only hope is Jesus, because it's plain as day to everyone but you that you are going to end up either in jail or dead."

"Just shut up, preacher man. I'm sick and tired of your Jesus talk, you freak." Jordan shoulder shoved him as he walked out of the men's room. After a few minutes, Paul headed back as well. He walked down a corridor and turned a corner to head back into the great room, where his office was over on the other end. He wasn't paying much attention, but when he glanced over towards his office, it

Chapter 3

almost seemed like Jordan had just come out of it. He watched as Jordan headed back to his cubicle, never meeting Paul's gaze. Once he sat down, he was out of sight behind his cubicle wall.

It occurred to Paul that he had left his monitor unlocked, and wondered if Jordan were malicious enough to delete his presentation. It didn't matter, Paul always kept a copy on a thumb drive just in case there were network issues and he had to use his backup. But if that were the case, it was a serious enough offense that he would have to tell Larry. At the very least Jordan would get written up, but that might actually be enough to fire the guy.

He got back to his desk and saw that his presentation was still there on his monitor, George Willow's business card and the meeting particulars were still on his desk, and it didn't appear that anything had been disturbed. Paul thought he must have been mistaken.

It was now 10:00 a.m. and the meeting wasn't until 11:00. It would likely go through lunch in order to accommodate George Willow's schedule. He decided to go down to the café on the first floor and have a light brunch to tide him over, so his rumbling stomach didn't interrupt the array of amber waves of American grain. He sat there leisurely for about forty minutes, eating a sandwich and chips, reading a newspaper that had been left on a table, then headed back upstairs.

Talks To A Picture Of Jesus

At five minutes till eleven, he headed out to the reception area so he could greet George and his people as soon as they walked in. He knew Susie would call him when they arrived, but he liked to start the ball rolling with personal attention. They hadn't requested lunch, which the firm would have gladly provided, so Susie had coffee, tea, and snacks ready for them there, and there were beverages and snacks in the conference room as well.

It was unusual not to wine and dine a client for weeks leading up to the presentation, but George Willow had made it clear that he would spare them this much time and no more. So, when 11:00 a.m. came and the Willow Grains team had not arrived, Paul thought it must be due to the man's very busy schedule.

At five minutes after, he still was not terribly concerned, but Larry came out to the reception area just then to find out what was going on. Ken and Larry always started off the presentations, before turning it over to the campaign manager to run the Power Point, and there would be a few other staffers there, ready to spring into action should something not go just perfect. Susie had not yet called Larry to come out to greet them, so he decided to see for himself.

Larry asked Paul to call the Willow Grains office and see if he could find out their status, and headed back to his office. Paul started to go to his

Chapter 3

office to place that phone call, but some unknown force had him turning towards the conference room instead. He wasn't sure why he thought he needed to check it, but he did. That's when he saw Jordan in the conference room with three men, who he assumed were George Willow and his team.

Paul bristled as he realized what Jordan had done. "Gentlemen, I'm Paul Hilliard. Thank you so much for coming today. Jordan, that will be all. I will take it from here. Hello George, nice to meet you. I'll get Ken and Larry in here, and we'll get started."

Jordan had packed up his documents and turned off the projector as soon as Paul walked into the room, and was at that moment heading out of the conference room without any sort of explanation.

"What do you mean, get started?" George Willow asked, then continued, "Jordan said Ken and Larry would not be able to make it and insisted that we come at 10:30 instead of 11:00. We've already seen the presentation and hated it."

Paul replied without any hint of being flummoxed, "Gentlemen, I'm afraid there's been a miscommunication. I'm not sure why Jordan had the wrong information, but Ken and Larry are right down the hall and will be here momentarily. I don't know what presentation you saw, but Jordan must not have been in the loop and didn't know that it was

Talks To A Picture Of Jesus

my presentation we would be showing you today. Is there anything I can do to get you to stay just a little longer and show you what we have in mind for Willow Grains? I've studied your mission statement and your demographic and would hate for us all to miss this opportunity while you're all here."

Without showing it, Paul was desperately trying to keep a bad situation from heading worse. Jordan had gone way too far this time, between the drugs and deceiving George Willow into viewing his own presentation, he had no doubt Larry would have to fire him now. It was hard to be sad for a guy like that. Miraculously, George agreed to stay for Paul's presentation, and once they got everyone in the room, it went off without a hitch.

Towards the end, George said, "I have to say, this was a lot better than that first one. That first one looked like a fifteen year old had produced it. Not bad Paul, I think you've captured the essence of what Willow Grains is all about. Ken, Larry, I think it's safe to say we can get the lawyers involved now, and start working on a contract." Ken and Larry had no clue what George meant about the first presentation, but they were ecstatic that Norris and Tuney had snagged the Willow Grains account.

It wasn't until after everyone dispersed that Paul pulled Larry aside and told him what had happened. Paul had been right about Jordan coming out of his office, just not about the intent. He had at

Chapter 3

first thought that Jordan had done something to sabotage his presentation, but now he realized that Jordan must have obtained George Willow's contact information from his desk in order to call him and convince him to come in early. He surmised that Jordan must have let the men in through the back employee entrance, which is why Susie had not known they were there. Larry was so angry that he set off for the great room to fire Jordan right then and there, but Jordan was nowhere to be found.

Chapter 4

Talks to a Picture of Jesus

Thankfully the gym wasn't very crowded that Tuesday evening. Tuesdays didn't seem to be a very big workout night, so Josie never had to wait very long for machines to become available. She liked to warm up on the treadmill, then rotate machines to workout arms, legs, and abs before finishing off on the elliptical.

Besides herself, there were three men using the weights, and a couple who were also using the machines. She really was trying to mind her own business, but the man of the couple was making it very hard, and Joy had not referred to Josie as a firecracker for no reason.

The man kept berating his wife or girlfriend, whatever she was to him, calling her fat, calling her stupid, cursing at her, and just being the most obnoxious thing anyone could imagine. Josie was trying to ignore him, but her sense of outrage at injustice got the better of her, and she was getting madder and madder with every hateful word.

Chapter 4

"Maxine, you can't do anything right. Your hands are in the wrong place, you're not sitting up straight, and you lift like a girl. Could you be any stupider?"

For some reason that Josie could not comprehend, Maxine actually apologized to him and said, "I'm sorry. I'm doing the best I can Eddy! I just need more practice, and then I'll get it right." He would occasionally crack what he thought were jokes about the fat old broad, and the old ball and chain, and look over at the weightlifters to see if he could get a laugh out of them, but he was oblivious to the fact that they did not consider his jokes funny at all.

Finally, the woman said she was done and headed off to the girls' locker room to change. Josie waited until she was out of earshot before saying to him, "You're a horse's butt, you know that, right?"

"What's it to you, little girl? Mind your own business, and nobody gets hurt."

Planting her hands on her hips, Josie spat back, "I was minding my own business until you made yours so very public. You're going to reap what you sow, and I wish I could be there to see it."

Eddy yelled towards the locker rooms, "Maxine! Get out here now, we're leaving! They forgot to take the trash out here." He gave Josie a sideways glance, and then headed out to reception to wait for her.

Talks To A Picture Of Jesus

Josie hoped and prayed that he was just a hot air balloon and not physically violent with Maxine. She remembered the verse that says human anger does not bring about the righteousness that God desires, and hoped her actions had not made it worse. 'Lord, if Maxine needs help, please do something, anything to help her,' she silently prayed.

When Maxine came out of the girls locker room, Josie intended to ask her if she needed to go to a safe place, but one of the weightlifters beat her to it.

A young black guy stood up and said, "Lady, your man's a jerk, and you deserve better. You don't have to be with a man who treats you like that, no woman should. If he abuses you, please let me take you to a shelter. My mom went through that with my dad, and it made me mad that I couldn't do anything as a kid. So, if I could help you now, it would be an honor."

Maxine was very surprised at this, but then she didn't know about the angry exchange between Eddy and Josie. She furtively looked over at the reception area where Eddy was waiting. "I do want to get away from him, but I can't do it here, and he won't let me drive. Can I call you later and pretend to order a pizza? Then I could give you my address. He won't think anything about it if I wait for you

Chapter 4

outside. He checks my phone all the time, so I'll have to disguise it."

The man agreed and gave her his phone number, which she quickly put into her cell phone.

"Thank you!" she said to him as she went to meet Eddy.

The young man then turned to Josie and said, "I want to thank you for speaking up. I was feeling pretty ashamed of myself that I was letting him talk to her like that. I was a kid all over again remembering what my dad did to my mom and feeling like there was nothing I could do. But when you called him a horse's butt, I thought to myself, 'how come little miss pint size over there can call him out but you sittin' here like you don't see what's going down?' I'm not going to be that guy anymore, I'm going to get involved and maybe like, I don't know, volunteer or something. God bless you ma'am."

He walked out, and Josie was so very glad that it seemed God had indeed been at work in this situation. 'Thank You Lord,' she thought, 'thank You that You took something bad and brought about good. Only You could do that!'

The rest of her workout was blissfully quiet and uneventful. She never showered there at the gym. It looked clean, but she didn't want to take any chances. So, when she was done, she stayed in her stretch pants and baggy tee-shirt and headed home.

Talks To A Picture Of Jesus

Linda's dress didn't need much more than hemming now, plus some appliques and beads along the hem. So, she decided to rest a bit instead of working on it that evening.

"Oh wait," she said to the picture on the wall, "We've got Awanas tomorrow night, and Chloe is coming on Friday which means I won't be able to work on it this weekend. Drat!" Realizing the rest of the week had activities planned, except for Thursday night, she went ahead and ran down to get the dress out of the trunk.

She turned the TV on for a little noise as she worked, and the news of a fatal hit-and-run accident was being reported at that moment. "Oh my goodness, how awful!"

Someone had hit a parked car, while a pregnant woman was retrieving something from the trunk. Witnesses said the driver was going way too fast, and had apparently lost control of the vehicle, hit the rear driver's side of the lady's car, killing her instantly. She was rushed to the hospital where they performed an emergency C-section to try to save the baby, but were unsuccessful. The reporter said that the driver of the vehicle, when found, would be facing two counts of vehicular homicide.

"What a horrible thing to have to live with!" She looked at the picture on the wall again and said, "Lord, please help that family! I don't know if she had any other kids or a husband, but I know she had

Chapter 4

parents, and they just lost their daughter and grandbaby. Please be with them, and send somebody to love on them and to be Your hands and feet. Wow! And whoever was driving that car, please let the police find him or her so that justice can be done. And whoever it was, they're going to have to live with that forever now, so please help that person to turn to You for forgiveness." She didn't say amen. Her conversations with the picture on the wall were just that – conversations.

Her morning prayer was always on her knees at her bedside, and always directed toward God the Father. Throughout the day, she very often included Him in her thoughts in sort of a "pray without ceasing" attitude. But in the evening, she liked to talk to the picture on the wall. She didn't know if it bore any resemblance to Him or not, but what she really liked about it was that He looked Jewish in this one. Many other pictures had been painted or sketched where the subject did not even remotely look Jewish, but this new one actually did.

So she had regular conversations with this one, hoping that He didn't consider it idolatry. She didn't think He would, because she knew that He was sitting on His throne, not inhabiting the picture, but she had heard other Christians claim that it was idolatry.

Nevertheless, it comforted her a great deal to have these conversations with Him. She could

Talks To A Picture Of Jesus

pour her heart out to Him much more deeply than she could with her mom or Chloe, or she could just ramble on and on about nothing, just like she could with her best friend. He was, after all, even more her best friend than Chloe was. So late at night, when all is quiet and still, she talks to a picture of Jesus.

The rest of the afternoon was very relaxing for everyone but Larry. Not only did the tension melt after a much anticipated presentation, but Jordan wasn't there to stir the pot either, and arouse resentment.

Larry, on the other hand, was on his cell phone much of the afternoon screaming at Jordan's voice mail. Jordan had never once picked up, nor did he return any of Larry's calls. All the great room staffers were secretly amused that Jordan was finally getting his comeuppance, and smiles were on every face.

At 5:00 p.m., Paul headed home, and quickly found himself in bumper-to-bumper traffic. He had plans to play basketball with Mark and some of the men of the church, and was afraid he might have to

Chapter 4

cancel on them. But then again, some of them might be in this traffic, too, so they would probably just start a little later than expected.

He turned the radio on, but instead of his usual Christian music stations, he hit a preset for a local all-talk station, hoping there might be some news as to what the traffic was about. A few minutes later, his curiosity was appeased with the news that a fatal accident had occurred along his route.

"For those of you just tuning in, we've got a traffic alert for anyone using or planning to use the Jefferson Parkway, both North and Southbound lanes," said the radio announcer. *"An expectant mother was hit by an out-of-control driver who immediately fled the scene. The body has been removed by ambulance, but police are still on site collecting evidence, so expect delays for probably about another hour. We'll keep you posted, though, with our first-alert sky cams, so stay tuned...."* Paul turned the radio off. "Oh man, that's too bad" he mumbled.

Much of the world was quickly becoming desensitized by the constant news of tragedy, riots, hate crimes, and terrorism, and Paul saw this as a loss of humanity. God made us to be compassionate, and instead, too often a blind eye or a closed ear is all that is proffered. So to guard against desensitization, Paul said out loud as he was

Talks To A Picture Of Jesus

driving, "Father God, I don't know who she was, but You do. You know her family and how much they are hurting. Please be with them. Comfort them in such a way that they know it's from You. Amen."

Just then, his cell phone rang over his car speakers via Bluetooth, and the console screen told him it was Mark calling. Paul answered the phone by saying, "Hey buddy, I may be a little late."

"Yeah man, that's why I'm calling. I figured you were on the JP stuck in traffic right about now," Mark replied.

"It's bumper-to-bumper. I guess there was a really bad accident and someone was killed."

"I know, I heard. The guy didn't even stop to see if she was okay. He just took off."

Paul asked, "Did they catch him yet?"

"I don't think so. As far as I know, they still have an APB out. A traffic cam caught a partial plate, but he must have had that silicone spray on it because it was really fuzzy. At least, that's what Tom says," referring to an officer who attended Mark's church. Mark continued, *"My wife didn't know her, but she knew of her, and I guess they're members of Parkview Baptist out on the East side. I went ahead and called over there to see if our church could help out."*

"Oh that's great. I'm glad to hear it."

"Anyway, Wayne's stuck in that traffic, too, and Smokey was one of the first responders, so he'll

Chapter 4

be late tonight as well. If the guys all still want to get together, why don't we just plan on 8:00 p.m. instead of 7:00?"

"Yeah, that'd be fine. That will give me time to stop and get some groceries so I can actually eat before I get there."

"Ha, ha, ha, the joys of being a single dude! Don't worry buddy, we'll get you a wife one of these days."

They hung up, and Paul wondered how different life would be with a wife. He actually liked to cook, but he didn't like to go grocery shopping. He considered it a good trade off that he would prepare the meals if she would do the shopping, He wasn't looking for a slave, just someone to do life with, someone to love, honor, and cherish. Most importantly, though, he wanted someone who was already walking with the Lord, so that it would just be natural that they walked with Him together.

He saw a quote a long time ago, and Googled it to see who said it, but wasn't able to find its origin. It went something like 'a woman's heart should be so hidden in God that a man has to seek Him just to find her.' He was seeking God with all his heart, and trusted that one day, God would reveal that special treasure.

Basketball is always a great night out. It was cathartic for Paul to be able to forget about work, forget about Jordan, and just shoot hoops with

Talks To A Picture Of Jesus

friends. But it was late, and most of them had wives who were expecting them home.

Paul pulled into his garage and entered his house through the laundry room, tossing the keys in a bowl when he got to the kitchen. He turned on the lights, but not for very long. He just wanted to talk over the events of the day with the One who had seen it all, and knew it was coming; so he sat in his recliner and swiveled to face a bookcase instead of the television.

"Well, this was an interesting day. I sure was sorry to see what Jordan was doing in the bathroom. He's wrecking his life and he doesn't even know it. And that stunt he pulled," he said, shaking his head. "Thank you for working it together for good anyway. You're pretty awesome. Ha, ha, and that mouse was funny, thanks for that too. Larry needs Your help figuring out what to do about Jordan. So would You mind helping him out? All in all though, it was a good day. And I guess every day is a good day because You made it, and You make all of it to work together for my good, don't You? Even the ones I think are bad days." He yawned and stretched his arms before continuing. "It's time for bed, so I'll see you tomorrow. Goodnight."

With a slight nod at the frameless picture propped up against some books in the bookcase, he got up and turned the lights off, then headed down the hall. This was a regular thing for Paul. Late at

Chapter 4

night, when all is quiet and still, he talks to a picture of Jesus.

Chapter 5

Girls' Day Out and Guy's Day Busted

Nearly simultaneously, both girls screamed, "Josie!" and "Chloe!" when Chloe finally arrived at the shop at 1:30 Friday afternoon. Josie didn't mind, she knew Chloe well enough to know that she wouldn't be there by noon. She wondered how Chloe ever made it to court on time, but there was probably a big difference between professional Chloe and personal Chloe.

She had passed the bar a few years ago, and was now a junior associate with Tuttle, Jones, Horowitz and Mann, practicing, of all things, banking law. Growing up, Josie never would have guessed that Chloe would eventually become a lawyer, or that she would choose a career in banking law. Her exciting and inquisitive nature might have led her into criminal law, where she could solve mysteries and cases at the same time, but Chloe was full of surprises and definitely not predictable.

The two girls were miles apart, and had formed an unlikely friendship, but it was one that was born out of heartache, so it had firmly stood

Chapter 5

throughout grade school, junior high, high school, and college. Chloe's dad had left the family when she was seven years old, leaving her, her alcoholic mom, and her three-year-old little sister to fend for themselves. Her mom had had a series of boyfriends in and out over the years, and it was not uncommon for Chloe to show up at school with bruises. Her little sister had eventually gone to live with distant relatives, but Chloe wasn't wanted because she was age nine by then, and the relatives felt she was no longer malleable and would be too much trouble.

Since she was a frequent visitor at the Montgomery home, Joy and Joseph had sought legal counsel to make Chloe a part of their family, but it was a different time back then, and CPS hardly ever removed children, even when physical abuse was evident. Joy and Joseph also suspected sexual abuse, but were never able to prove it or get Chloe to talk about it. So, they did the best they could by letting Chloe stay with them for as long as her mother would let her, and made her an unofficial part of their family. The structure and discipline were good for her, but she was still very much a wild child, and together, the girls got into their fair share of trouble.

When Chloe got pregnant in high school, she secretly went to a clinic and had the baby aborted. Everyone saw a change in her after that, as Chloe increasingly became depressed and irrational. It was

Talks To A Picture Of Jesus

almost a relief when Chloe checked herself into a rehab center, but still a shock.

She was still underage and could not get ahold of her mom to come down and sign for her, so she did the next best thing and called the Montgomerys. It had been a very difficult decision for them to let her stay there. They wanted more than anything for her to come home with them and get counselling from their pastor, but Chloe was adamant that she wanted to be there for just a little while to get her head together.

While the Montgomerys were signing the financial responsibility paperwork, Josie had had a chance to talk to her best friend.

"Was the baby Van's" referring to Chloe's boyfriend.

"Yeah, it was his," she responded dejectedly.

"Did he know? Is that why you guys broke up?"

"Yes. He called me a slut and said there was no way he would marry me."

"Ugh, what a jerk. Chloe, why didn't you tell me? We tell each other everything."

"I know," she sighed. "I just couldn't bear the thought of your mom and dad being so disappointed in me after all they've done for me. And I didn't want you to have to keep it a secret from them. I'm so sorry, Josie! I really messed up!"

Chapter 5

Chloe laid her blond, curly head on Josie's shoulder and sobbed.

Josie thought how easily it could have been herself in this position. Josie was not living a godly life and she knew it.

"Chloe, maybe they're right. Maybe you should just come home with us and get counselling from our pastor."

"No! He would judge me and make me feel even more horrible than I already do! All I want to do is stay here for a week or two and get all this junk out of my head."

Josie shook her head and said, "I don't know much about it, but I don't think it takes a week or two. And he's not like that, you know, you've met him."

Chloe pleaded, "Josie, please, just let me do this. I'll be back to normal soon, I promise. And all this will just be a bad dream. "

"Alright, I won't bug you about it. I just hope you're doing the right thing."

That was the beginning of Josie's own personal inner reflection. A couple of other things happened in high school that caused the self-examination to continue, so that by graduation, Josie had decided to stop sitting on the fence and live for the Lord in earnest.

Joy, who was in the back room working on the week's receipts, heard the commotion and came

Talks To A Picture Of Jesus

to greet Chloe as well. Hugs abounded, and the ladies began the catching up process over at the coffee bar in a corner of the boutique. Although Sylvia was there helping customers, every now and then one of them had to stop and answer a question, or rescue a toddler who had put his hand in a vase, and in general, be mindful of the store. So Joy said at length, "You girls need to scoot on out of here and go do something fun. Sylvia and I can manage for the rest of the day, so be off with you," waving her hands dismissively.

That was fine with them, they were happy to spend the rest of the day enjoying each other's company. But Chloe looked around the shop for a little while before leaving.

"Where do you get all this super cool stuff?" she said, as she stroked the velvet of a plush purple pillow decorated resplendently with an oriental-looking elephant. It was propped up in a Queen Anne style chair that Josie had purchased at a garage sale and reupholstered in turquoise and gold paisley-patterned chenille, with a black feathered boa draped over the back and side of the chair.

Above it was a plaque that Josie fashioned out of old fence boards she had found in an alley. She had stenciled the famous love passage from 1 Corinthians in big red letters –" Love is patient, love is kind. It does not envy, it does not boast, it is not proud. It does not dishonor others, it is not self-

Chapter 5

seeking, it is not easily angered, it keeps no record of wrongs. Love does not delight in evil but rejoices with the truth. It always protects, always trusts, always hopes, always perseveres. Love never fails." For the letter 'o' in the very first "love" she painted a crown of thorns rather than a plain old 'o', and the letter 't' in the word "truth" was a medieval cross.

"I sewed all the pillows, and all the clothes except for the hats. I made some of the crosses, the fabric and wood one, but not the metal ones. I refinished a lot of the furniture pieces in here, including that chair. The furniture itself comes from garage sales, thrift shops, and antique stores."

Chloe praised her, "Oh my gosh, Josie, you are so clever! How come your craftiness never rubbed off on me?"

Josie laughed, "I seem to recall you were pretty good with a can of spray paint!"

"Ha, ha, ha, I was, wasn't I? And now here I am, upholding the law!" She was referring to their youthful criminal activities when they had graffitied the dog house in Josie's backyard.

When Joseph Montgomery discovered them, his initial reaction was anger, but the terrified looks on the girls faces softened him, and he decided it was a good idea to paint the doghouse. So although they hadn't planned on it, under Joseph's supervision, they continued spraying until all the

Talks To A Picture Of Jesus

graffiti was covered up and the doghouse looked brand new.

All the while, Joseph talked about the importance of being a good citizen, respecting other people's, and other dog's, property, and lending a helping hand wherever a need comes to light.

Josie said, "Why don't you pick something out and it will be my gift to you."

"Seriously? Cool! I do really like that pillow."

"Then it's yours," Josie replied as she picked it up to put it in a store bag. She added, "It's too late in the day to go garage-saling, but do you want to go antiquing with me? The shops close between 5:00 and 6:00 p.m. so we would be able to hit a few, then go back to my apartment and you can get ready for your meeting tonight. But we'll come back here first to get your car."

"Okay, I would love to see things from your perspective, and find out what beautiful treasures you're able to imagine in what I would probably think of as junk. Ha, ha, look at us, antiquing! Just like an old married couple."

They enjoyed a very nice rest of the afternoon, and Chloe was truly impressed with Josie's vision of what several items could become. At a thrift shop, they found an old canoe that was obviously no longer water worthy and Josie said, "I would attach braces on either side so that it stands

Chapter 5

upright, then screw in shelves to make a bookcase. Then, just paint it really nicely, and it would be great for a man-cave." It didn't match the more feminine theme of the boutique, so she didn't buy it, but a couple nearby overheard her and looked at each other with a little bit of wonder. When Josie and Chloe moved away, the man picked it up and took it up to the counter.

Josie found several items in that short shopping excursion, and pulled out the company credit card each time, with her name emblazoned on it and Jay Jay's Boutique underneath it. At the last store, as she was making her final purchases, Chloe reached over and took her wallet in order to examine the modifications Josie had made. It was a denim covered wallet, to which Josie had added red lace and ribbon.

"Cute!" Chloe said. Meanwhile the cashier handed back Josie's credit card, and since her wallet was otherwise occupied, she stuck it in an outside pocket of her purse, intending to put it back in her wallet, probably when she got home.

Shopping completed, with a break along the way for an ice cream cone, they headed back to get Chloe's car. On the way, Josie asked, "Are there any interesting men in your life right now?"

Chloe laughed and replied, "Well there's a guy at the law firm who has asked me out on a date, but guess to where?"

Talks To A Picture Of Jesus

"Where?"

"To his Church! Ha, ha, ha, ha, ha! Who does that? Who asks a girl to church for a first date?"

Josie sort of rolled her whole head, not just her eyes, and said, "A good guy, Chloe! The kind of guy I'm looking for, that's who!"

Chloe laughed again and said, "Fine, I'll introduce you to him. No, not really."

Josie's eyes threw darts at her. "Why!?"

"I don't know," Chloe shrugged, "maybe I want to save him for myself. He's cute and I like his company. He doesn't make me feel like a skank."

"Oh my gosh, you are not a skank! You're not, are you?" Josie said with a sideways glance.

Chloe shrugged again, "Some people think so. But not Rick. He really is a nice guy. I can't see us together, though. I mean like, you and me, we're best friends, but we're not going to get married, so it's okay that you're religious and I'm not. I think if this guy really knew me, he probably wouldn't want to hang around me anymore."

"Chloe, I love you, and God loves you. And it's okay to not be religious, He wants you to turn to Him exactly as you are now. And because I love you, I know that you are worthy of love. Someday, I hope you realize that. And as for this Rick guy, you could do a lot worse than a guy who wants to take you to church instead of to bed."

Chapter 5

Chloe looked as if she were really thinking about what Josie said, instead of dismissing it flippantly, the way she usually did.

They got Chloe's car and headed back to Josie's apartment so Chloe could change. When Chloe came out of the spare room dressed in a black sequined mini dress with a plunging neckline, Josie said, "Whoa sista, isn't that a little over the top for a client meeting?"

"Relax, it's a cocktail party, remember?"

"Yeah, but wouldn't you still want to look professional, like a lawyer? What if your client gets the wrong idea?"

"Don't be silly, Josie. I know what I'm doing and this will be fine. And I brought something demure for Sunday," she said with more sarcasm in her voice than was necessary.

Josie rolled her eyes and replied, "Oh, well there's that, I guess."

"I'm going to be pretty late, so would you mind either giving me a key or leaving the door unlocked?"

Josie asked suspiciously, "What are you not telling me, Chloe?"

For the briefest moment, Chloe's eyes flashed a little tiny look of panic, before setting her face on neutral. Turning to her best friend with a smile, she replied, "Nothing, you worry wort." Josie

Talks To A Picture Of Jesus

felt very safe in her apartment complex, so she was okay with leaving the door unlocked.

"Don't wait up!" her best friend said as she walked out the door.

The red flags had Josie turning to the picture on the wall. "Please keep her safe!" she pleaded.

Paul didn't go to the gym on Fridays because he enjoyed a break from his routine. His goal wasn't to become muscular, it was just to stay strong, in shape, and hopefully avoid any more of the "dunlap" disease that had started to set in when he turned thirty – when the gut "done lapped" over the belt. He was a big guy, but not abnormally so, bigger than Matthew McConaughey but not as big as Dwayne "The Rock" Johnson.

On Fridays, he usually made himself a Southwestern omelet for breakfast before heading into the office. Jordan hadn't been in since the fiasco on Tuesday, and he wondered if they had seen the last of him. He didn't think so, because Jordan had finally called Larry back late Tuesday evening to let him know that he had been in an accident Tuesday afternoon, and played on Larry's

Chapter 5

sympathies. Larry pointed out that if Jordan had been at work, where he was supposed to be, the accident would not have happened. But Jordan didn't know that he would have been fired that day anyway, and Paul wasn't sure if Jorden knew that today was originally supposed to be his last day either. It wouldn't surprise him if Larry had caved.

It had been a productive few days without Jordan's constant disruption, and in the relaxed atmosphere, Paul had come up with a few new ideas for some of his clients. He was looking forward to working with Victor on some mock-ups in order to prepare a few pitches. When Paul got to his office, he read his daily online devotional and the corresponding scripture, then committed his day to the Lord.

At 8:00 a.m. as usual, the office began filling up and there was a general "Happy Friday!" feeling in the air. Paul turned on his radio and rolled the dial to Air1®, hoping to catch some Skillet and make the atmosphere even peppier. But at 8:15 a.m., there was a slight groan throughout the cubicles as Jordan walked in and took his seat. He did it quietly, instead of greeting them with, "Hey losers!" but it had still thrown a wet blanket over the office.

Paul turned off the radio to see if he could hear the explanation as to why Jordan had been missing for the last two and a half days, but strangely, there wasn't any talking at all. Jordan was

Talks To A Picture Of Jesus

unusually quiet. After about forty minutes, Paul got up to stretch his legs, and headed out to reception to say hi to Susie, and to let her know that his 2:00 had emailed to say he was starting the weekend off early and needed to reschedule. Susie wouldn't need to have the snacks and beverages out and ready as a result.

Paul was there chatting with her when two uniformed police officers and a man in a suit walked in. The three of them showed their badges and the man in the suit introduced himself as Detective McPherson, and the officers as Officers Corley and Adams.

"Ma'am, we're here to see Jordan Tuney. Would you be kind enough to escort us to wherever he sits."

Susie said apologetically, "Oh, I can't leave the desk, but I'll call him and tell him to come up," reaching for the phone.

Detective McPherson said authoritatively, "Ma'am, do not pick up that phone. He is not to have any advance notice that we are here." He also looked at Paul, indicating that he must also follow his instructions.

Susie's eyes grew big and her hand slipped back to her side. In a scared voice, she said, "I'll call Larry and see what he wants me to do," and slowly reached again for the phone.

Chapter 5

With a little exasperation, Detective McPherson said again, "Ma'am, again, under no circumstances are you to pick up that phone and alert anyone inside to our presence. Simply show us where he is, and we'll take it from there."

Eyes wide, she looked at Paul for help and Paul jumped in with, "Gentlemen, I'll escort you inside and take you to Jordan myself."

"Thank you sir, lead the way."

The presence of the officers in the great room caused a stir and heads started popping up over the cubicle walls to see what was going on. Paul led the officers up to the cubicle at the end, where Jordan had his head down, pretending not to notice, but all the while with an angry scowl on his face.

Paul stepped back so that he was not in their way as the uniformed officers each placed a hand on Jordan's shoulders, then with their other hand, they each grabbed a wrist, pulling it around to Jordan's back and at the same time lifting him out of his chair. As they were doing this, Detective McPherson was saying, "Jordan Tuney, you are under arrest for the murder of Juliana Stevens and her unborn child. You have the right to remain silent……"

As he continued reading Jordan his rights, Larry came bounding out of his office, his face covered in pure disbelief. "Jordan! What did you do!"

Talks To A Picture Of Jesus

"Sir," said Detective McPherson, "I need you to step back. I'm sure you have a lot of questions, but right now, you need to let us do our job."

Larry, still in a state of shock, looked at Detective McPherson as if he were an alien from another planet. "I'm his uncle, Lawrence Tuney. What did he do?"

"It's an open case and we can't say a whole lot about it, but did you hear about the accident on the Jefferson Parkway Tuesday afternoon? Or read about it in the paper?"

Larry looked at Jordan in even more unbelief, if it were possible, and said, "That was you? You killed that pregnant woman?"

Jordan, who had been looking down in silence the whole time, finally looked up at his uncle, and where there should have been remorse on his face, there was only bitterness and resentment.

Then he looked at Paul and said, "I guess you got your wish, preacher man. Now you can spread your phony religion all over the office without me here to enlighten these stupid losers."

This was not the time to get angry. Actually, it didn't even occur to Paul to get angry, this was too serious of a situation. "It's not too late, Jordan. Jesus would save you even now if you were to ask Him; not from the consequences of what you've done, but He would save your eternal soul from damnation."

Chapter 5

Detective McPherson added as they started leading Jordan out of the office, "You'd better listen to him, son. God is your only hope, and although you're in a world of trouble right now, He can turn your mess into a message."

And with that, Jordan was out the door and out of their lives for the foreseeable future. Larry couldn't help it. His sagging stance needed support, so he leaned against the wall and started bawling. His beloved brother's only son had committed a heinous crime and the grief of it was overwhelming. Paul put his arm around Larry and helped him get back to his office, shutting the door behind them.

Paul was about to help Larry into his chair, when Larry suddenly turned to Paul and grabbed the lapels of Paul's blazer.

"Paul, you've got to help me pray for him. Please help me. When I talk to God, all I know are memorized prayers, but when you talk to God, you're really *talking* to Him, like you're communicating with Him. You've got to help me do that. I just can't believe Jordan….." His words trailed off as his voice choked in another sob.

Without a word, Paul helped Larry onto his knees right there and took Larry's petition before the Lord. "Father God, You see the brokenness and You long to reach down with healing and forgiveness. And You would forgive Jordan if he would just turn to You and ask for it. This is awful,

Talks To A Picture Of Jesus

Lord, this is just awful, what he's done. Please have mercy on him. Jesus, knock on the door even louder. Father, please draw Jordan to Your Son. Holy Spirit, please put such a strong conviction on him that he can't bear it anymore and turns to You. Lord, You see Larry's broken heart, too. Please comfort him in such a way that he knows it's from You. Help him to remember that, as much as Larry loves Jordan, You love Jordan even more. Please Lord, bring something good out of this mess, so that someday, we can all look back and say, 'look at that, God did that.'

And Lord, I pray for the family of Juliana, I forgot her last name. I ask for comfort for them, too. Mark said they were members of Parkview, so hopefully You are loving on them through their church and through our church. Thank you for being bigger than our faults, hurts, problems, tragedies, everything. Your Word says You can do everything and no one can thwart your plans, so please bring good out of this awfulness. And once again Lord, please do a miracle inside Jordan. This is important, so we're asking this in Your Son's name. Amen."

Larry, who was encouraged by the natural way in which Paul was speaking to his unseen God, added his own prayer. "God, Jordan's a screw-up. I know that, You know that, but somehow he doesn't know that. Please have mercy on my stupid, idiot nephew. He looked like he didn't even care about

Chapter 5

what he'd done. He's such a moron! But You can fix him! I know You can! Please fix him! Amen."

They got up off their knees and Paul, who was facing the door, saw that a few people had been watching. But they scuffled off before Larry saw them.

Larry said, "Thank you, Paul. That part about asking for comfort for me and knowing that it came from God – He put you in this office for that very reason, and for this very moment. I'm pretty sure of that."

Paul was touched. "Thank you, Larry. Is there anything else I can do to help?"

"Nah, I think I'll head over to Parkview and see if they can get me in touch with the family. I've got to tell them how sorry I am."

Paul had plans with Mark after work, so when he met him at the batting cages, he told him everything that had happened, not out of gossip, but because Mark already knew some of the inside details from a police officer and a firefighter in the church, and the pastor at Parkview.

Mark said, "I think Larry was right. God probably put you there for such a time as this," referring to Esther 4:14. "God directs our steps and puts us where He wants us in order to fulfil His plans, not only for our lives, but also for His kingdom work. That office, Larry, and Jordan in particular, have been your mission field. Keep it up Paul, you're making a difference."

They spent the rest of the evening mostly in silence, but Mark tried to lighten the mood every now and then with a bad-dad joke.

Chapter 6

Get a Tissue and Laugh a Little

Josie didn't know if she should stay up for Chloe or not, but the decision was made for her at 9:00 p.m. when Chloe called her cell phone.

"Josie, I need you to come get me." Chloe's words were slurred and had to be repeated for Josie to understand.

"Okay, which hotel are you at?" Chloe told her and Josie flew out the door. She didn't know why Chloe's words were slurred, but instinctively knew it was bad, and probably not due to alcohol. Chloe never let the drinking get away from her because of her alcoholic mother. She saw firsthand the truth behind the happy-go-lucky, party-time false front on strong drink, and knew that it was really a viper waiting to rise up and strike. Chloe had many vices, but excessive drinking wasn't one of them.

Josie pulled into the hotel parking lot and gasped, "It's Van!" Chloe was trying to get away from her old high school boyfriend, but she was no match for him, especially in her current state, and he

89

Chapter 6

was forcibly pulling her across the parking lot back to the hotel.

Josie gunned the car straight towards them, stopping just short, and Van was caught in the glare of the headlights. She jumped out of the car and threw her pointed forefinger in his direction, yelling, "The Lord rebuke you!"

He was caught off guard by all this and tripped over a concrete parking barrier, going down very hard. That was Josie's chance to pull Chloe into the safety of her car. She sped away before he could get up.

Chloe was softly crying. "I think he put something in my drink. I wasn't even going to have anything, but he wouldn't take no for an answer."

"Chloe, what was Van even doing here?"

"He was the one I was meeting."

"As a client?"

"No."

After a few seconds of silence, Josie asked, "As a booty call?"

"Yes." The simple admission floored her. Why was Van still in her life after all these years?

Josie thought it wouldn't be long before Chloe was unconscious, so she pressed a little more.

"Have you seen Van before tonight?"

"Yes. A long time ago, he told me he was sorry and that he wished he had married me. He was already married but said he would leave her. I

Talks To A Picture Of Jesus

was so stupid. I believed him. But he stayed with her and then a year later, gave me that same song and dance. Every man I've ever known has always wanted one thing, and I guess that's all I'm good for. That's what one of my dads even told me. That's all I was good for to him, too."

Josie felt sick to her stomach. She knew her parents had suspected sexual abuse, but Chloe had never confided that to Josie. Josie brushed away the tears that were impairing her vision and said, "Chloe! That's not all you're good for! Oh baby, I'm so sorry you had to deal with that evil! You were just a kid! Oh God, please help!"

"God doesn't want me, He's ashamed of me. I've done even worse."

"Honey, that's not true. He loves you and there's not a single thing He would not forgive if you asked Him."

Chloe was silent for a little bit. "I wasn't going to go through with it this time. I had debated about it all the way up here, and when I got to the hotel and saw him, I knew I couldn't do it." Her voice shook with what she was finally admitting. "I told him I wasn't staying, and I think that's when he put something in my drink. He distracted me with some stupid story about seeing someone famous, and I turned my head to look, but he was full of it. I felt funny, and I knew I had to call you. Thank you, Josie." She was saying all this in between sobs, and

Chapter 6

Josie was continually wiping her own eyes and nose, trying to drive safely home.

"We have to go to the police, Chloe."

"No, I just want to go back to your apartment. Please, Josie, please let's just go back tonight."

"You know he will do this to someone else. He probably has already. There's no telling how many women he may have raped, and we have to stop him."

"I know, but right now, I just want to sleep." She was struggling to stay conscious, and Josie was nearing the apartment. There was no way of knowing whether it was Rohypnol or GHB, and if it were GHB, it would not be in her bloodstream in the morning. She prayed that it was Rohypnol.

Chloe passed out as soon as Josie was able to get her to the couch, so Josie did her best to arrange her in a comfortable sleeping position, took her shoes off, and covered her with a blanket. Then Josie went to kneel at her bed where she could cry good and hard to the only One who could do something about this.

It was a little while before she could even speak, but when she was able, she said, "Oh Lord, Chloe has been dealing with this since she was a kid." A little more crying, and then, "Please, please help her! She doesn't think You want her and that so breaks my heart! Please Lord, she desperately needs You! She needs to feel Your agape love, and she needs healing. Please, please, I beg You, please help her."

After a bit of nose blowing, she called her mom. "Mama, you and daddy have got to pray your heart out for Chloe right now." Joy put it on speakerphone so Josie could relay the evening's events to both of them. They had known Van when he was a teenager and were incensed by his reprehensible behavior.

Josie did not tell them about the abuse Chloe endured as a child, but she did tell them that she said she felt like all she was good for was sex, and that God could never love her. Joy started crying, wishing she were there to hug and comfort her pseudo-adoptive baby girl.

Josie could also hear the emotion in her dad's voice. "Sweetie, your mom and I will get down on our knees and pray all night, if that's what it takes. And as for Van, Joe Ford is the manager at that hotel, and it just so happens, he owes me a favor. I know they have security cameras all over the place, so I'll get him on the horn and get him to watch the recordings. If he can see Van putting anything in her drink, she won't even have to go to the police. They will start an investigation based on that alone."

Josie took a deep breath. "Thank you, daddy. You always know what to do."

Chapter 6

She tried to get some sleep, but it was fitful, and in the wee hours of the morning, she heard Chloe crying so she got up to check on her. Chloe must have been either crying in her sleep or immediately went back to sleep, because she didn't rouse when Josie whispered her name.

She pulled the coffee table out to give her room to lay down on the floor beside the couch, not wanting to leave her friend's side. Not knowing exactly what to do, and wanting to do something, she started softly singing, "Jesus loves you, this I know, for the Bible tells me so. Little ones to Him belong, they are weak, but He is strong. Yes, Jesus loves you. Yes, Jesus loves you. Yes, Jesus loves you, the Bible tells me so."

It was Saturday, so there was no alarm blaring in the morning, announcing the start of the day. When Josie opened her eyes, it seemed to still be very early, based on the soft glow of light behind the sheer window curtain. She looked up to see if Chloe were awake. Chloe was now laying on her stomach, with her feet propped up on an arm rest, and her head and one arm half on the couch and half dangling off. Her eyes were still closed.

Josie got up to check the time on her phone – ten minutes till seven – and saw that she had two text messages that her mom had sent late last night. **Joe checked the security footage, saw Van put something in her drink and pulling her across**

Talks To A Picture Of Jesus

parking lot. Police went out, got copies, started an investigation.

The second message read, **They will want her to go down for a blood draw, but it's enough already to pull him in for questioning.** Josie was relieved to read that an investigation had already begun. She hoped Chloe would cooperate and give them a sample of her blood. She texted back, **Thanks Mom, she's still asleep. Keep praying.**

She didn't feel like getting ready for the day yet, and actually, wanted to be there when Chloe woke up, so she followed up the text with, **Not sure how the day will go, may have to reschedule Linda's appointment. Will you let them know what's going on?** She knew her mom would already be up, so it wasn't surprising when the response came almost immediately, **Will do, sweetie.**

Josie turned on her stereo, low enough to hear clearly, but not loud enough to be an annoyance, and laid back down on the floor beside the couch. Within a few minutes, a song of redemption began to play.

I am guilty
Ashamed of what I've done, what I've become
These hands are dirty
I dare not lift them up to the Holy One

Chapter 6

Josie, who thought Chloe was still asleep, was surprised to hear Chloe say, "My hands are dirty." She held up the hand dangling off the couch as if to inspect it.

Josie softly responded, "Jesus can wash them for you."

> *You plead my cause, You right my wrongs*
> *You break my chains, You overcome*
> *You gave Your life to give me mine*
> *You say that I am free*
> *How can it be?*
> *How can it be?*[iv]

"Josie?" Chloe asked hesitantly, "Do you think babies go to Heaven?"

Josie thought of the baby Chloe had aborted when she was a teenager and wondered how she should answer. In a split second, she said in her mind, *Holy Spirit, help!* As honestly as she could, and to the best of her knowledge, she said, "We don't really know, Chloe, but we think so. In the Old Testament, David said he would see his son again in Sheol, and in the New Testament, Jesus said the Kingdom of Heaven is made up of children. I personally believe they do." Josie waited a second, hoping and praying this was finally the moment.

"Are you thinking about your little baby in Heaven?"

Talks To A Picture Of Jesus

Chloe shuddered with the strong emotion she was feeling. "I'm thinking about all four of them."

Josie did her best to not let the shock of that statement cause her to overreact and ruin the moment, but eyes wide, the tears were streaming down her temples, into her hair. "All four of them? What happened? When?"

"In college with one of my professors, then at the law firm where I interned. I got rid of them, too. I don't know why, I just did. I didn't want anyone to know that I had slept with a professor and an employer. That's what skanks and sluts do." She softly cried before adding, "That's why I know God doesn't want me. The last one, I was going to keep it. It was a boyfriend's and we ended up breaking up, but I was going to keep it, and it died. Josie, it died! God was mad at me!"

Neither of them could hold back the tears, one out of regret and one out of sorrow.

"No, Chloe, it doesn't work like that. This whole world is under the curse of sin and God loves you, and wants to free you from that curse! And Jesus died to free you from that curse!"

A song of invitation began playing on the stereo, and it seemed to Josie that it was perfect timing, so she let the words fill the room and do the talking.

Chapter 6

Are you hurting and broken within?
Overwhelmed by the weight of your sin?
Jesus is calling
Have you come to the end of yourself?
Do you thirst for a drink from the well?
Jesus is calling

O come to the altar,
The Father's arms are open wide
Forgiveness was bought with
The precious blood of Jesus Christ

Leave behind your regrets and mistakes
Come today, there's no reason to wait,
Jesus is calling
Bring your sorrows and trade them for joy
From the ashes a new life is born
Jesus is calling

O come to the altar,
The Father's arms are open wide
Forgiveness was bought with
The precious blood of Jesus Christ[v]

"Do you really think He can forgive me?"
"I know it, Chloe! There's nothing He won't forgive, you just have to ask." Again, the gentle tones of the next song wafted over the airwaves and

seemed to be perfect. Josie felt that God had ordained it to be so.

> *I see shattered You see whole*
> *I see broken You see beautiful*

"I'm scared. This broken life is all I know."
"Don't be scared, just surrender."

> *But You're helping me to believe*
> *You're restoring me piece by piece*

"What if I can't do it, Josie? What if I'm too dirty?"
"Don't worry, Jesus will wash you white as snow."

> *There's nothing too dirty*
> *That You can't make worthy*
> *You wash me in mercy, I am clean*

"Are you ready, Chloe?" It was evident that Chloe was in tremendous turmoil.
"What if I'm not good enough? What if He rejects me? How will I know?"
Josie promised her, "He won't reject you. He said 'Anyone who comes to Me, I will never turn away.'"

Chapter 6

Chloe was so close but still wasn't convinced. "But what if I can't change? What if I can't be good enough?"

Josie assured her, "That's not your job, Chloe. Your job is just to put your trust in Him. Give Him all your baggage and He will gladly take it. When you ask Him to save you, in that instant, you will become a brand new person, and *He* will begin to change *you*. In an instant, your spirit will come alive, like a light bulb is turned on, and then over time as you grow in Him, He will help you make better choices, and you'll have this amazing peace! I'm not saying it's easy, but I am saying it's worth it! It's so worth it, Chloe, to be at peace with God, to know that you're forgiven! Please say you're ready!"

Chloe could scarcely speak, so she nodded consent. Josie could hardly believe her dear friend was finally surrendering. She said through tears and sniffles, "Then tell Jesus now. Ask Him for forgiveness. Ask Him to save you."

Washed in the blood of Your sacrifice

"Jesus, I'm ready. Please forgive me!"

Your love flowed red and made me white

"I need You. I need You to save me."

Talks To A Picture Of Jesus

My dirty rags are purified, I'm clean

"I want to be clean!"

I'm clean! I'm clean!
You make me, You wash me, clean[vi]

"Oh wow!" Their tears were completely unchecked now. "I'm forgiven, Josie! I can tell! I'm forgiven! Wow, wow, wow, wow! I feel so light, like I could just float! It's so weird!" Tears now mingled with laughter and hugs as the weight of years of sorrow, hurt, sin, rejection, and abuse lifted from Chloe's heart. It's a transformation one has to experience to understand, but when someone does experience it, it's life changing.

They stayed where they were for about another hour, talking through the wonder of salvation and new life.

At length Josie said, "We're going to have to find you a good church so you can get baptized, then start learning and growing. You didn't have the benefit of Sunday School, except for those times you came with me, so we've got to get you connected with other believers in your area who can help you make sense of spiritual matters. You don't realize it, but you're vulnerable right now, and I'm going to get my shield and sword out, and pop and chop, and slice and dice those wolves." She was pretending to

Chapter 6

hold a sword and shield as she said this, and started fighting and kicking imaginary demons.

Chloe was laughing so hard that she said, "Stop it! I have to pee!"

"Oh man, you and me both!" was Josie's response. "Let's get ready and go down to the shop to tell my mom the good news. I have to do the final fitting for the wedding dress, so I'll have her call Linda to come meet us there. Then we'll have the rest of the day to ourselves."

"Deal."

Josie's apartment was a two bedroom, two bath, so they didn't have to share a bathroom and could get ready at the same time. But first, Josie texted her mom with the good news. In all caps, she wrote, **MOM, IT FINALLY HAPPENED! SHE GOT SAVED!** Joy's immediate response was, **HALLELUJAH!**

When they were both back out in the living room, Chloe said, "Would you hate me if I said I wanted to go back tonight so I could go to church with Rick tomorrow? In fact, I really want to call him and tell him I gave my life to Jesus." Chloe's smile and eyes shone so brightly as she said this that Josie's heart was bursting.

"No, of course I wouldn't hate you! But I would like to know the name of his church. I've got to check it out, you know," Josie laughingly replied, however she did really mean it. She wanted to make

Talks To A Picture Of Jesus

sure Chloe got started in a good Bible-believing church.

Chloe dialed Rick's number and when he picked up, Josie listened to their one-sided conversation with interest. "Hey Rick, it's Chloe….. I'm good. So, I have something to tell you. I asked Jesus to save me a little bit ago."

There's something about a smile that changes your voice. Anyone could hear the smile in Chloe's voice, and Josie assumed whatever he was saying back, it was very good. "I know! Isn't it great! …….. Okay …… Are you serious? …… Oh, thank you!" She whispered to Josie, "He's been praying for me." Into the phone she said, "So, is it okay if I go to church with you tomorrow? ……. Awesome!"

A little bit of a shadow clouded Chloe's face at that moment, but she continued, "Rick, I really need to tell you something. I have a past and I want you to know up front, because you might not even want to be my friend once you know everything."

Josie was so proud of her best friend's courage in sharing her story with Rick, and she was also surprised that she was sharing all of it. 'She must really like this guy', Josie thought.

When she was done, Chloe said into the telephone, "So what do you think, will you still be my friend?" Chloe listened attentively to Rick's response, and Josie hoped and prayed that he was being kind and supportive. For a minute or two, she

Chapter 6

only heard, "Really? …… Oh wow! …… How did you get clean, did you go to rehab? ……. What is Teen Challenge? …… What did they do? …… That's so cool! ….. Alright …….Thank you! Okay …… Okay, I'll see you tomorrow then,"

"Get the name of his church," Josie called out.

"Oh wait, Josie wants to know the name of your church." Chloe told her, and Josie had heard of it, remembering that the pastor was a well-known author, and felt her best friend would get a good biblical foundation there.

"Okay, thanks again, Rick, and I'm really looking forward to seeing you tomorrow."

She hung up and said, "Guess what? He has a past too, and he totally accepted mine. He said that he felt like God specifically wanted him to pray for me, so he has been, ever since we met."

"Oh my gosh, look at you, Jesus saved you and apparently gave you a good man all in one day!"

Chloe was supremely happy. "I'm still so floored. I don't know if anything will happen with me and Rick, and I don't even care. I can't believe he said he's been praying for me all along."

Josie said emphatically, "God has been pursuing you, Chloe. You didn't think He wanted you and he's been *pursuing* you!" she said, placing weight on the word pursuing. That brought a new wave of tears to their eyes, and both of them had to

Talks To A Picture Of Jesus

wave their faces because they didn't want to ruin their makeup.

When Josie and Chloe walked into the shop, Joy was there waiting for them. She put both hands over her mouth and then held out her arms. "Oh Chloe! Come here, baby!"

Chloe embraced Joy tightly and said, "Can you believe it, Mrs. Montgomery? I gave my life to Jesus!"

"Of course I can believe it! Our God is wonderful, and loving, and forgiving, and He put us in your life because He desperately wanted you to come to Him. Oh thank you so much, Lord, for answering our prayers for Chloe."

Ernestina and Linda were also there and added their congratulations. The dress was now safely in Linda's hands, final payment was made, and Josie felt like she could die happy right at that moment.

After Linda and her mom left, Joy said, "Girls, we have inside information that the police went to Van's house late last night and confronted him about putting something in your drink," looking over at Chloe. "I guess he must have gotten scared witless and confessed. It was GHB. They took him in and booked him for attempted rape, but he lawyered up. They are hoping that when the story gets out, women will come forward, but they've at

Chapter 6

least this to go on. Honey, I'm so glad he didn't get far enough with you."

"Me too, Mrs. M. Me too. I guess I'll call and see if I need to make a statement or something. GHB doesn't last long in your system, so they probably won't want a blood sample."

Chloe was very glad the video existed. It had crossed her mind that with a past like hers, no jury would believe she was innocent in all this. They grabbed a bite to eat before heading back to the apartment, and Chloe packed up to head home.

At the door, they embraced one more time and said, "I love you so much!"

"I love you too!" When Chloe was out of sight, Josie shut the door and turned to the picture on the wall. She clasped her hands to her chest, and for about the hundredth time that day, the tears freely flowed once more. "I am so incredibly glad. I cannot thank You enough. Thank you, thank you, thank you, Jesus."

Paul looked down at his plateful of eggs, bacon, sausage, hash browns, and pancakes and said, "I have a feeling my eyes are too big for my

Talks To A Picture Of Jesus

stomach, but I'm going to try to do this some serious justice."

Mark laughed and said, "Hey, did you know we have Spanish milk up there?"

"Spanish milk, where?" Paul looked around for this apparently exotic beverage.

"Up there, with all the rest of the coffee and stuff," nodding towards the beverage table.

"What makes it Spanish milk? Did you get it from Mexican cows?"

"No man, it's soy milk. Get it? It speaks Spanish. Yo soy milk! Ha, ha, ha, ha, ha!"

Everyone at the table laughed when they realized Mark had pulled another bad-dad joke on them.

"Mark, seriously, you're not going to have anything left for the competition," Paul chided.

"Don't worry, buddy, I've got thousands of them. I'm going to blow you all to smithereens!"

One of the young guys piped up, "Smithereens, is that even a word?" More laughter ensued at his expense. Good naturedly, though, he added to the conversation, "Why don't eggs tell each other jokes?" Before anyone could answer, he said, "Because they'd crack each other up!"

Everyone chuckled again, and Mark said, "Good job, dude! You're on the right track. We're making a bad-dad joke teller out of you and you're not even close to being a dad." Then pointing his

Chapter 6

finger at the young man, he added, "At least you'd better not be."

The young guy blushed and quickly replied, "Yes sir. I mean, no sir! I'm not going to be a dad for a long time, and I swear I'll get married."

It seemed like all fun and games, but Mark was pretty serious about teaching the teenage boys to live holy and pure lives. "Now Paul, on the other hand, Paul's going to be a dad any minute now."

Paul had just taken a drink of orange juice. Big mistake. In his shock, it went spraying toward the man across from him, plus the men on either side of him got a little doused. It was hilarious and everyone busted up laughing. Thankfully those men had started earlier than Paul and had already finished their plates, but Paul was in too much shock to be glad about it.

"What? Do you know something I don't know?"

Mark found Paul's reaction supremely funny. "Ha, ha, ha, ha! I'm kidding. But I do have something to tell you afterwards. What have you got going today? Do you have to be somewhere right after this?"

Paul was very curious at Mark's cryptic words, and answered, "I'll stay as long as you want. I'm going to fix a lawnmower for one of the girls at work, but I don't have to rush out for that."

Talks To A Picture Of Jesus

"Alright, it won't take long. I think we're about ready to start so I'm going to head up to the front."

There were a number of things they always prayed for at men's prayer breakfast; first and foremost was to spread the Gospel in their community. They prayed for their city leaders, then out further to their state government, then out even further and prayed for the federal government.

They had a list of the missionaries they supported, and prayed specifically for five of them on the list, along with their mission fields. In two weeks, at the next men's prayer breakfast, they would pray specifically for the next five on the list.

They also prayed, by name, for five children in their church, and likewise, two weeks later they would pray for the next five on the list. They called this method Five for Five – first: salvation, if they hadn't already been saved; second: obedience in believer's baptism, if they hadn't already been baptized; third: that they would walk with the Lord all their lives; fourth: that they would be witnesses; and fifth: that they would cultivate the Fruit of the Spirit. It was a program that was sweeping throughout churches all over America, and they were grateful that their church had a heart for children, because they believe Jesus has a heart for children.

Chapter 6

They also had various prayer requests that had been called in throughout the week, along with praises for answered prayer. Finally, they ended in typical fashion with several of the men going up to lay hands on Mark, as many as could reach him, and prayed that Mark would remain strong in the faith, pure in his marriage, and withstand the attacks of Satan. Mark had never asked for this, and he was so humbled that his men did this for him.

Afterward, the men usually chitchatted for a long time before dispersing. It was sort of funny that on Sunday's, they complained about trying to get their wives out the door because of the visiting and chitchatting, but every other Saturday, when they did it, it was called "fellowshipping."

Mark and Paul finally had a moment to talk, and Mark said, "So are you a little worried about what I said about you being a dad soon?"

Paul laughed, "I wouldn't say worried, but I am definitely curious as to why you said it."

"Ha, ha. I was just kidding about that, but I do want to tell you about my prayer time last night. Look, I know we said we were only going to pray once for you a wife, but you came to my mind last night, so I went ahead and asked God to give you someone really special. I told Him most importantly she had to be walking with Him," then he jabbed Paul with his elbow, "but that it wouldn't hurt if she were nice to look at, too. And you know what?

Talks To A Picture Of Jesus

What popped into my head at that moment was 'Love is patient.' I started thinking about that, and how it might apply to your situation; and the more I meditated on it, the more it seemed like the Lord was saying she's out there. But the kind of love you're wanting takes patience, and this is part of whatever plan He's working on for you. And maybe it's for her, too. I don't know, like maybe she has to fulfill her part in His plan. Is this making any sense? Anyway, that's all it was. Love is patient. I just felt like I needed to tell you, buddy."

"Alright, thanks Mark."

"No problem. Hey, but when she finally shows up, you'd better call me first, man."

Paul chuckled, "Will do."

Chapter 7

The God-incidence

Josie was still in high spirits Monday morning as she pulled out onto the Jefferson Parkway. Yesterday had been a fabulous day in the Lord's House, between the music, the message, and sharing Chloe's salvation with those who remembered her from their youth. Her dance threshold was even lower than usual, and pulling up to a light just as Audio Adrenaline was singing *I get down, You lift me up*[vii] was a good thing, because it meant she could clap her hands after the *Down* beat and pop them up right on that *Up* beat without having to hold the steering wheel.

When her eyes veered over to the traffic on the opposite side, she had a sense of déjà vu when she saw a silver Explorer, and then a shock when she realized the guy in the explorer was once again keeping time with her, only this time, unlike last time, he was aware of her.

He was grinning as he watched her gyrate to the music, and when he caught her eye, he started playing an air guitar. She belly laughed, and would

Chapter 7

have continued this theatrical display, but the light changed at that moment, and cars started moving forward. So, she waved at him and cruised ahead.

Once at the shop, she started looking around the backroom at all the inventory to be painted, refinished, blinged, and/or otherwise worked on. It was a relief that the wedding dress was done so she could refocus on these forgotten treasures. It had been an exciting adventure, but it was so time consuming that she didn't think she'd take on another wedding dress for a long time. "Unless it's my own," she cupped the side of her mouth and whispered loudly to the blue and gold brocade she was measuring for a storage bench.

"Your own what, honey?" Joy had come in either very silently or Josie had been too deep in thought to hear her.

"Ha, ha. I'm busted. I was talking to the brocade."

With a tiny hint of sarcasm, Joy replied, "I figured that out, dear, but I didn't hear the first part of that conversation you were having with that apparently highly attentive material."

She laughed again and admitted, "My own wedding dress. I told it I wouldn't take another order unless it was my own. I loved doing Linda's but, holy cow, I'm glad it's over. Except, I may have to make one for Chloe. She was positively sparkling whenever she talked about Rick."

Talks To A Picture Of Jesus

"Would you be okay with that, Sweetie? I mean, if Chloe got married before you did?"

Josie thought for just a second before saying, "I think so. I've got a really good life, Mom, and I almost think Chloe needs marriage more than I do. She needs that stability and unconditional love. I super hope she finds that in Rick, but it's way too soon anyway. She probably needs to grow a little first. They would not be unequally yoked now, but they are still not in the same place yet, either. Rick has a head start in his walk with the Lord."

With a bright smile, she continued, "We'll see. I'm still just so unbelievably happy she got saved on Saturday." At that, she did a little jig, throwing her hands up twice with a "Whoop! Whoop!"

Joy laughed and said, "You and me both, honey. Oh, the gray hairs that girl gave us! God really does work miracles. But that reminds me, I've been meaning to tell you to be on guard for the next few days."

Josie looked puzzled. "What do you mean? For what?"

"Well, whenever these spiritual victories are won, the enemy is furious. So, put your armor on and be on guard for an attack. They'd like nothing more than to put you in a tail spin and see you come spiraling down. Capiche?"

Chapter 7

Her use of the word 'capiche' had Josie holding out her hand, fingers and thumb together Italian style, and replying in her best Chef Boy-Ar-Dee accent, "Yes-a ma-ma. I capiche. Oooo, that reminds me," quickly and unintentionally changing the subject. "I saw a really cool metal suit-of-armor statue at the store the other day. It was only about four feet tall, and more than I wanted to pay, but I thought it would be really neat to do a whole medieval-ish, Armor of God-type display. We have enough medieval stuff that I bet I could really do it right. Even like this brocade, this would be great!"

As Josie rambled on, Joy hoped her daughter comprehended what she was trying to tell her, and watch out for attacks, because they could be very subtle, or they could be overt, you just never know. But she had complete faith that God would get her through it, if it happened.

Josie was so pumped about her upcoming Armor of God display that she began rearranging items in the store, looking for anything gothic. If she went ahead and bought that suit of armor, she could put it on a Plaster of Paris Corinthian capital she found at a craft store, and that would bring it up to about five feet. She had a plethora of gothic crosses, a couple of metal candlestick holders that would suit the display nicely, and a Jacobean-style chair that she had painted black. She could make a seat cushion for it out of that lovely brocade.

Talks To A Picture Of Jesus

"It's going to be so cool!" It was a little more manly than she was used to creating, but she could envision someone wanting the entire display for a man-cave. Somehow she would have to tie it all together with the verses from Ephesians 6 so people would understand the concept.

She looked around the shop to get ideas on how to showcase the Scriptures, and her eyes fell on her stenciled fence boards adorned with the love passage from 1 Corinthians. When she is not dealing with customers and has time to think about it, she sometimes looks at it and asks herself, 'Is Josie patient? Is Josie kind? Does she envy and boast? Is she proud? Does she dishonor others? Is she self-seeking? Does she keep a record of wrongs? Does she delight with evil or with truth? Does she protect, trust, and hope? Does she persevere?' It's a sobering thought, and it causes her to think about her interactions with people, and where she might have prevailed or what she could have done better.

No one is perfect, everyone has their something, and there were times when she felt like she failed miserably. But there were other times when she could look back and realize she had gotten it right – when she had said the right thing, or kept herself from saying the wrong thing, had helped out a homeless man instead of passing him by. The little things add up, and nothing that is done for the Lord is done in vain. So, she committed this display to the

Chapter 7

Lord and asked Him to cause it to be a blessing to someone.

The day seemed to fly by, with plenty of customers to fill each passing minute. Josie's good mood lasted all day, and because she frequently thought of Chloe, several times she broke out into song.

"You make me feel like dancing," she sang to a little boy who smiled wide before hiding behind his mom's legs. Then he would poke his head out to look at her, and she said "Boo!" each time.

When they left, she looked at the clock – ten minutes till four. Josie felt like she would get a good workout that evening and was hoping Sylvia would be a little early. Someone else came in just then, so she looked around to greet her new customers.

"Hi. Feel free to look around, and let me know if you need anything."

Her customers were two young women, one was taller, wearing jeans, a tee-shirt, and sporting a boyish haircut, while the other young lady was in a mini sundress. They were holding hands, but Josie didn't need the visual to know they were a couple. She frequently had girls come in together, and treated them like everyone else.

The taller girl said to the shorter, "This isn't our kind of store, Lori, let's go."

Lori replied, "No, let's just ask, Doreen. It can't hurt to ask."

Talks To A Picture Of Jesus

It wasn't really eavesdropping since Josie was only about five feet away, so Josie said, "Ask me what?"

Lori took the opportunity to pull away from Doreen and take a few steps toward Josie. "We saw on Facebook that you made a wedding dress for a girl we went to high school with, and want to know if you will make one for me."

Josie shook her head and replied, "No, I'm sorry but I just can't take another special order right now. But you can take a look at what I have over there on the rack, some would be really nice for a wedding, unless you're set on white."

Doreen huffed, "I bet you would take one for your cross-y friends," holding her fingers up in air quotes.

Josie's smile did not reach her eyes as she said, "Look, that was hard work and I need a break. I may not even do another wedding dress ever again, I don't know yet."

Doreen, however, was undaunted and said threateningly, "If I find out you took another wedding dress order for one of your Christian friends," again with the air quotes, "I'm going to sue you."

Josie's immediate reaction was anger, but she still managed to keep it mostly in check, considering they were customers. Tersely, she replied, "You can try, but when I win, I will be asking

Chapter 7

for attorney's fees. Ain't nowhere on that door where it says bridal shop. It's not my specialty. I did Linda a favor, mainly because her mom and my mom are good friends. But it's over now and I need a break. It was exhausting."

Doreen was not convinced. "You people are all hypocrites. You make me sick."

In a split second, because that's all it takes, Josie remembered her mom telling her to be on guard. She remembered her earlier desire to show patient love, and she acknowledged God, in order for Him to direct her path right at that moment – all of that in a split second. Her reply wasn't nearly so terse this time as she said, "Have you heard that joke, where do sinners go?"

Doreen answered, "Phbbt, we go to hell?"

Now softly smiling, Josie said, "No, we go to church."

Doreen chuckled and looked confused at the same time, so Josie continued, "What better place is there for sinners than church? We are all hypocrites of some sort, because we all wear a mask. We hide behind what we want people to see, and we pretend like we're all that and a bag of chips. All of us do it, Doreen. But inside, we all have something going on that we don't want anyone else to see. You know who sees? Jesus sees. Jesus told a story one time about two guys who came out of church at the same. It was really the temple, but let's call it

Talks To A Picture Of Jesus

church. Anyway, one guy looked really good. He had on a suit and tie, was clean-shaven, and he was probably good looking. When this guy came out, he stopped to pray out loud so that everyone could hear him. He said 'God, I'm so glad I'm not like other men. I give money to the church, I give money to the poor, I do all sorts of good things. I'm so glad I'm not like that loser over there.' He was talking about the other guy who had come out of church at the same time. This other guy wasn't in a suit and tie, his clothes were baggy and dirty, and I don't know, he may have even smelled bad. This guy was in the same service, sang the same songs, heard the same message, and Jesus said this guy was so convicted that, in humility, he wouldn't even lift his eyes up to Heaven, but instead, beat his chest and said, 'God, have mercy on me, a sinner!' Jesus said that's the man who went home justified. Yes, you're going to find hypocrites at church, and that's okay because he needs to hear Gods word too. Who knows, maybe he'll change someday. But you're also going to find those of us who know we're sinners and want God to change us. Doreen, let me tell you about my best friend, Chloe. The most amazing thing happened this weekend."

There's something about pure joy that's contagious, like a baby's smile. It takes the sourest of sourpusses to resist smiling back, and the kind of joy that lights up a face also brightens a room. So as

Chapter 7

Josie was describing how Chloe gave her life to the Lord, her joy spread to Doreen and Lori, even though they didn't know it. They were smiling back, except it was still a confused smile, as if it were another language, but a pleasant language.

Josie's mom had still been in the backroom when this started, but she heard the initial threat and got up to listen at the door, all the while praying God would use Josie for His glory. She was passing the test.

Josie was now finishing up and said from the deepest part of her heart, "That's what it's like! It's awesome! It's a love that you just can't believe, but it's real! I have it, and now Chloe has it, and you can have it too! What do you think? Do you want it?"

Doreen shook her head as if coming out of a trance. "No. I don't buy it. Come on Lori, let's go."

No one had seen that Lori had covertly set her sunglasses down, and she didn't pick them up when they left. Joy came out of the back room when the front door closed and threw her arms around her daughter.

"Josie, I'm so proud of you! You handled that really well. That could have gotten very ugly, but you did good, sweetie!"

They heard the front door open again and Lori stepped back through. "I forgot my sunglasses," she said, reaching for them. "And I just wanted to say thank you. Doreen can be such a pill sometimes,

Talks To A Picture Of Jesus

but you were really nice. She likes to provoke people, and we've been thrown out of a lot of stores."

Josie asked gently, "Does she treat you okay, Lori? Does she ever try to control you?"

"Not really," was the hesitant answer. "I have to go. Thanks again."

"You're welcome! And if you ever want to talk, come back and see me."

"We'll see. Bye."

The door closed behind her, and Joy and Josie prayed together that God would water the seed planted in them, and that He would draw them to His Son. Sylvia arrived shortly after that, and Josie was very glad to get away. She had gotten to witness again within two days, and it was the best feeling in the world. She was going to have a really good workout that night.

Yes, it was a good workout that Monday night. Josie had stamina enough for probably three times her normal routine, but settled for twice so as not to overdo it.

Happily exhausted and thoroughly sweaty, she grabbed a towel from her locker to dab her face. She also changed into a spare pair of stretch pants and tee-shirt out of consideration for her car seats, then took her purse down from the hook at the top of her locker. Still with towel in hand, and that same

Chapter 7

joyful smile on her face, she walked out of the locker room swinging her purse and humming a tune.

When she got to the reception area, where new members sign up for their initial contract, she put the towel to the corner of her eye to dab a little more sweat and ended up swinging her purse against the front desk, bumping it sort of hard. In fact, it was hard enough for the boutique credit card, which was still in a pocket because she had forgotten to put it back in her wallet, to slip out, hit an edge, and bounce under the desk, with just a corner peeking out. It was carpeted in the reception area, so she never heard it, and because she was dabbing her eyes at the time, she never saw it. She was still happily humming when she walked out, leaving her credit card mostly hidden, but still slightly exposed and at risk to anyone with evil intent.

Tuesday morning, Paul woke up with a Sunday school song in his head. 'This is the day (this is the day), that the Lord has made (that the Lord has made). I will rejoice (I will rejoice) and be glad in it (and be glad in it).' The children's choir had put on a special performance during last Sunday night's

Talks To A Picture Of Jesus

service, and Paul had an earworm now, that chewed away at his brain. There were definitely worse things in life, so he let it go round and round as he worked out Tuesday morning. It made his bench presses more enjoyable as he lifted to the beat.

He thought about Mark's joke that he would be a dad soon, and found himself pleased with the thought of a son to throw a baseball with, or a sweet little daughter to dance on his feet. 'Slow down, dude,' he rebuked himself. 'Love is patient.'

He thought about the various single women at church, and although they were all nice and wonderful in their own way, he wasn't particularly interested in any of them, which was a good thing, really, considering none of them paid much attention to him either.

He wondered if he had ever missed any cues from any of them, because so often he'd been told that men are clueless. That didn't compute with him because in his estimation, there wasn't a single thing men missed about women. They noticed everything, in his opinion, from polished toenails to the shine of their hair. 'But it's true we don't understand them, and probably never will. Oh well, put it out of your mind, boy-o, time for a shower.'

He began to go over his projects for the day: a conference call at 9:00 a.m. with Willow Grains; a staff meeting at 10:30. He needed to check on Victor and see how he was coming with his concept

Chapter 7

sketches.   Then, later that afternoon, he had an unusual appointment.

A commercial they were doing for a chain of shoe stores had to be recast because the CEO didn't like the walk of one of the shoe models. Paul didn't have anything at all to do with the casting, or the filming for that matter. That was contracted out to a studio. So he wondered why Ken and Larry wanted him to go with them to the studio that afternoon. 'Maybe they are grooming me to become a partner. Things are looking up for you, Pauly boy.' He made a click sound on one side of his mouth as he pointed at himself in the mirror.

Shaving done, toiletries put away, clean clothes on, it was time to go. At 7:00 a.m., Paul walked out of the men's locker room and back out through the weight room. His phone beeped at him, indicating a text message, so he pulled it out and was reading the message as he entered the front reception area. It was just a reminder that his cable bill was about to be drafted, so he deleted it.

He turned the screen off and was about to put his phone back in the case on his belt, when something on the floor caught his eye. Because he had been looking down at the right time and right place, he saw the edge of a plastic card peeking out from the front desk. He reached down and retrieved it, and saw that it was a credit card.   "Josie Montgomery, Jay Jay's Boutique."

Talks To A Picture Of Jesus

It was too early for the guy who signs up the newbies to be there, and he didn't really want to leave it on the desk where anyone could get it. He went around and checked a few drawers, a little worried that someone might see him and misconstrue his actions, but the drawers were locked. So he pocketed the card and decided to call the lost or stolen number on the back to report that he had found it.

Chapter 8

The Big Day

Josie's alarm went off promptly at 6:00 a.m. Tuesday morning, but Josie did not immediately get out of bed to turn it off. She had been awake for the last fifteen minutes, however, the bed was warm and cozy, and she preferred to lay there and think about the events of the day before.

She thought of the girls who had been in yesterday afternoon, and Doreen's comment, "I don't buy it." She wondered if Lori would ever come back in to talk. She thought of the conversation with her mom about having a good life. 'I do have a pretty good life,' she affirmed. It was different than what she had expected, but it was still very good. 'This must be a good hormone day,' she thought. On bad hormone days, Josie rued becoming an old spinster. She wasn't even close to being a spinster, but on those days, it felt like it.

She decided to go ahead and purchase the four foot suit of armor she had seen at a nearby home decor store. It was a little out of the ordinary, both price-wise and design-wise, but she felt it

Chapter 8

would be worth it in the end. The beeping of the clock would not stop by sheer force of will, so Josie got up to turn it off.

Her prayer time was ever so much sweeter and she still marveled that God had been so incredibly kind to allow her to be the one to lead Chloe to Him.

After showering, makeup, and doing her hair, she put on her new black floral skirt and paired it with a pale pink knit shirt. Yesterday, in all the inventorying and rearranging of the store, she had come across some faux silk she had purchased months back, intending to whip up a skirt with it, but Linda's dress had put that thought on hold. So when she found it, she knew it wouldn't take long and decided to make an asymmetrical fishtail wrap out of it. A seam here, a seam there, a couple of darts, and it was done. She surveyed herself in the mirror and was very pleased with the fun hemline and the big pink and yellow flowers against the black material.

Driving to work, she smiled as she passed a certain intersection, thinking of air-guitar-guy. She didn't have to stop for the light, so there was no point in looking for him. She'd never see him again anyway. It was just a fluke.

The conference call with the Willow Grains Vice President of Marketing, Bill Yates, went fine,

Talks To A Picture Of Jesus

but was, in fact, premature and Paul hoped they weren't trying to pull a fast one. The contract was still with the lawyers, so it was really too soon to go over Paul's ideas and compare them to Willow Grains' expectations.

It had occasionally happened with a couple of other companies, that after a pitch was presented and subsequently rejected, commercials would pop up very similar to the ones that had been suggested by Norris and Tuney; and since they always applied for copyrights, minus any trademarked names, it brought about lawsuits.

Paul had to be careful about discussing anything other than the original presentation. If Willow Grains pulled the plug on the contract, Norris and Tuney would closely monitor their campaigns for plagiarism and/or violation of copyright law. Nevertheless, it had been an amiable conversation, and he hoped the contract signing would go off without a hitch.

After that, Victor came in with his sketches, and he and Paul worked on those for a while, tweaking here and there. It would all have to be redone digitally eventually, but he enjoyed working with Victor to get his ideas out on paper first. One other seasoned man also preferred Victor's sketches, but none of the young guys and girls did. 'The times, they are a-changing,' Paul thought. Paul wasn't even

Chapter 8

that old, but to the younger crowd, he supposed thirty-five was considered seasoned.

An email came in just then. *Sorry for the short notice, but the 10:30 staff meeting has been cancelled. Too many people are out with illness or are on vacation, so we'll reschedule it for another day.* That was just fine with Paul. It was an HR meeting to go over the paperwork required for their new health savings account administrator. Boring!

A doughnut sounded good, and now that he had time to go downstairs to buy one – 'Oh yeah, that credit card from this morning,' Paul remembered. He pulled it out and turned it over for the phone number. It occurred to him that he could just call the store and offer to return it. If she had already canceled the card, he would just put it in the shredder, but if she hadn't, it would save her the hassle of having to wait for a new card.

He would just arrange to meet her at the gym. So he googled Jay Jay's Boutique for the phone number and saw that it had a social media page. When he pulled it up, the first post he saw was of a suit of armor next to an oldish looking chair that you might see in an English manor, or maybe even a castle. Behind it was blue and gold material draped to form a curtain, and it was surrounded by gothic looking crosses, candlestick holders, and a chalice.

The owner, Josie Montgomery, had posted the following comment*: Ladies, be sure to come by*

Talks To A Picture Of Jesus

and check out my new Full Armor of God display, and consider gifting your knight in shining armor with this knight in shining armor. It would look great in his man-cave! Paul's whole house was a man-cave, so he wondered where he could put it. It was an interesting idea, and he liked the Full Armor of God theme.

Now he was curious, so he scrolled down to see more posts. There were various pictures of clothing that she had apparently made herself; chairs, benches, and footstools that she had re-covered; an armoire that she had stripped and refinished; some fence boards that had been cut down to approximately two feet by two feet and contained the words Love is patient, Love is kind.....

"What a coincidence!" Paul said to his empty office. He clicked on it to make it bigger and studied it. It was definitely feminine, but he liked the crown of thorns in the very first 'o' and the cross that made the 't' in truth.

He escaped out of the picture and clicked on the About page. There was a map of the store's location, and Paul saw that it was up the street from the gym. The store contact information was also there, but Paul was interested in what Josie had posted under the Story section. *Dad and I wanted to name the store Agent Jay's but Mom, in her wisdom, won out with Jay Jay's. Mom and I own and run the boutique together, and our only goal is to meet your*

Chapter 8

needs for interesting home décor and fabulous clothing. Our motto is 'Do all to the glory of the Lord.' Again to his empty office, Paul said, "Wow, that's really neat, you don't see that very often coming from a business owner." He picked up the phone.

Josie had wasted no time getting her new display together. She had Joy cover the store for a few minutes while she ran out to pick up the suit of armor. She was practically the first person there at the home décor store when it opened, so she was in and out in less than ten minutes. The armor and chair alone would never have made a decent display, but fortunately she had so many other items that happened to look medieval, that when put together in her own personal brand of flair, it looked fantastic. She took a picture of it with her phone and posted it on Jay Jay's social media page.

"Mom, come look," she called out to Joy.

"Oh!" Joy exclaimed. "Josie, I thought you were out of your mind when you suggested this, but I really like it! And if your dad could hobble down here to see it, he'd want the whole thing."

Josie laughed, "Dad doesn't have a man-cave, so you'd better hope it sells before he has you moving furniture around to make room for it." Joseph was scheduled for foot surgery shortly, so he was in no position to move furniture.

Talks To A Picture Of Jesus

She finished her post and silently said a prayer that it would go to a good home, and be more than just something cool and eclectic. She wanted it to be a reminder that we truly do need to put on our armor every day and do battle for the King of kings.

The phone rang a few minutes later and Josie called out, "I'll get it." The voice on the other end said, "Hello, I'm looking for Agent Jay."

"Ha, ha, ha, ha, ha! You've got her, unless you're calling for my mother."

"Oh, is she Agent Jay too? Which one is Josie?"

"That's me. Josie by day, secret government agent by night."

It was his turn to laugh. "You lead an exciting life. What do you call a secret agent running to catch a bus?"

In a puzzled voice, Josie answered, "Um, I have no clue."

Paul pulled out his best Sean Connery accent, which he hadn't used in years, "A Russian spy."

"Ha, ha, ha! Oh my gosh, that was corny!"

Paul chuckled, "If you think that's bad, what do call a frog spy?"

"Oh no, what?"

"A croak and dagger agent."

Chapter 8

"Ha, ha, ha, ha! So is this what you do all day, you call up random businesses and start telling jokes?"

"Absolutely! It's what I live for!" Paul responded. He added, "I've got a million of them. I'm practicing for a competition on Saturday."

Josie exclaimed, "How fun! A joke competition?"

"Even better, a *bad-dad* joke competition," Paul said, emphasizing the words 'bad-dad,' and quickly adding, "I'm not a dad yet, but I can't pass it up. It's going to be hilarious!"

Josie asked him, "Is that like those videos going around on social media, where they tell awful jokes and try their hardest not to bust up laughing?"

"Yeah, that's what we're doing. It's a community outreach thing at my church."

At this point, Josie still had no idea who she was talking to. "What church do you go to?" she asked. He told her, and she said, "Oh I know about that church. I've gone to a few of their Passion Plays and they were amazing!"

"Thanks," he responded. "We really try hard to bring in people who would not normally go to church, but might try these different venues. It's a great way of getting the Gospel out in a more relaxed atmosphere. I saw your Armor of God display on Facebook just now and I really like it."

Talks To A Picture Of Jesus

Josie was very surprised. "You're kidding, I just posted it like ten minutes ago."

"Great timing then, isn't it?" Now maybe it was starting to make sense.

"Oh, is that why you're calling?"

"No, it's not, but I do like the display and I think it would look sort of cool in my living room."

"Not your man-cave?" she said with a smile in her voice.

"My whole house is my man-cave. And by that I mean, bachelor pad, really. Hang on, that didn't sound right. Not a bachelor pad as in 'hey baby, come check out my crib' sort of place, it's just my house. It's a good thing you can't see me, because I think I'm probably blushing, ha, ha, ha."

Josie was still so confused with this strange man, but regardless, he was a potential customer, and a funny one at that. She shook her head and chuckled. "So let me get this straight, you're a joke-telling, church-going, evangelizing, bachelorizing kind of guy who is not a dad yet, trolling social media pages and making random phone calls to beautiful women in your best Sean Connery voice?"

Paul realized the absurdity of the situation. "Ha, ha, ha, ha, ha! Is this the strangest telephone conversation you've ever been in?"

"Yes! *Who are you?*" Josie couldn't hardly stand it anymore, the curiosity was killing her.

Chapter 8

"Ha, ha, ha! Let me start over from the beginning. Hi Josie, my name is Paul Hilliard, and I have your credit card."

"WHAT?" That was the last thing she expected to hear, so he finally explained.

"As I was leaving the gym this morning, I saw something under the desk up front, so I pulled it out and it was your credit card. It has your name and Jay Jay's Boutique on it. I googled Jay Jay's to see if I could get it back to you, and here we are."

Now she understood, "Oh! I forgot to put it back in my wallet on Friday, and it probably fell out yesterday evening when I left. Now I remember bumping my purse on the desk. Oh my goodness, thank you!"

"You're welcome. I wasn't sure whether or not you had already reported it as lost, so on the off chance that you hadn't, I thought maybe I could just give it back to you."

She was impressed by such consideration. "Wow, what a kind-hearted soul! Do you want me to come pick it up? Or can I meet you at the gym? It's almost lunchtime."

It was indeed almost lunchtime, and Paul had enjoyed his conversation with her. He wanted it to continue, so he risked rejection and said, "You're right, it is almost lunchtime. We could meet at the gym, or……. we could meet at the Chinese restaurant next door, and I could buy you lunch."

She was so startled that she stammered just a bit, not able to speak a complete word. He added quickly, "Unless there's a Mr. Josie who would beat my brains in for taking you to lunch."

Regaining her composure, she said, "No, there's no Mr. Josie, so…….. okay, I'll meet you there. Wait, you're not buying with my credit card, are you?"

"Ha, ha, ha, ha! Cross my heart, hope to die. I guess it's a date then."

He could almost hear her eyes grow wider as she said, "Okay, see you in a few minutes."

"Who was that, dear?"

"His name is Paul, but I don't remember his last name. He found my credit card at the gym. And now I sort of have a date to get it back. I'm going to meet him for lunch."

"Huh." Joy stood there looking at her daughter contemplatively for a while before finally turning to go back to the workroom. "Have a good time."

Before turning the key in the ignition, Josie sat in her car for a little bit and thought, 'How am I supposed to recognize this guy? I guess he'll be waiting for me. What if I get there first? Why didn't I ask what kind of car he drives or what he'll be wearing? Josie Renae, you numbskull! He could be a perv or a kidnapper! You could be meeting a serial killer for all you know!' Multiple questions ran

Chapter 8

through Josie's mind all the way to Lo Chen Den, the restaurant next door to her gym.

This was definitely a first. There had been occasional talk amongst her friends about setting her up on a blind date, but she had always laughed it off, telling them not to bother, that she wasn't really looking anyway.

And now, here she was heading towards her first blind date, with no references at all, just on the basis of a pleasant conversation. 'He sounded really nice though, and he goes to church, there's that. It may not mean anything though, a lot of people see it as almost a social club. But he was proud of their outreach ministries, so maybe he's for real? Oh Josie! It's not like you're meeting your future husband, he could be twice your age! You're just going to get your credit card back, and if something's wrong with him or you feel uncomfortable, just leave. Oh man, I should have arranged some sort of signal with my mom. I guess if I need to, I can always text her and have her call a few minutes later and tell me I need to go back to the store.' Her thoughts were all a swirl.

Paul recapped what he knew about Josie. 'Age? No. She sounded youngish though. Looks? No. But she referred to herself as beautiful. Christian? Based on her store's social media page, probably yes. Walking with the Lord? Again, based on her page, seems like a yes there too.' What had

Talks To A Picture Of Jesus

made him ask a complete stranger to lunch? Why didn't he just meet her at the gym? He knew why – it was her laugh. It was a natural laugh, not in the least bit forced, a little throaty, and at times completely unrestrained. Her laugh had been so engaging. Whatever may become of this adventure, he just wanted to meet the person behind that laugh, and if that was it, that was it.

Paul did arrive shortly before Josie, but not knowing what she drove, he looked in the restaurant window first to see if there was a lone woman waiting. Not seeing anyone, he stood in front of his car and watched the traffic, waiting for someone to pull into the parking lot. A car did, but it was a guy who headed into the gym for a lunchtime workout. Then a Ford Fiesta pulled into the parking lot, and Paul thought the car and the occupant looked slightly familiar.

Josie saw a guy standing outside of the restaurant and to the left, and wondered if that were him. She had to pass and park two spots further to the left, and as she did so, she noticed he was standing by a Ford Explorer, similar to the one she was interested in purchasing. It was also similar to the one she had seen twice on the JP, 'Wait, is that him? Oh my gosh!' She got out and headed towards him with a big smile and a look of amazement.

"Air-guitar guy!" was how she greeted him.

Chapter 8

"Yeah, and you're Lift Me Up girl," Paul said, popping his hands up a couple of times.

Josie tried to get out a complete sentence, but wasn't doing a very good job. "How on Earth? Who would have thought? What are the chances?"

Since they already had this strange connection, it seemed the most natural thing in the world to hug each other when they were close enough. She was surprised that he remembered the song that had been playing when they had seen each other across the intersection.

Had she known, she would have also been surprised that he liked the scent of her hair. 'A little peachy? Or maybe mango', he wondered silently. Out loud, he said "This is quite a coincidence, isn't it? Hi, I'm Paul Hilliard. It's really nice to meet you, Josie. Shall we go inside?"

Once they were inside and seated, he pulled out his wallet. "Here, here's your credit card, safe and sound."

"Oh, thank you, Lord!" was her initial reaction, but in case he was offended, she quickly added apologetically, "And thank you, too!"

He shrugged and said, "No, you're right. God should get our first thanks."

"I can't believe I didn't even miss it! Someone unscrupulous could have found it and had a great old time at my expense. I'm so glad it was you."

Talks To A Picture Of Jesus

"Me too. It is pretty amazing how He works, isn't it?"

"Absolutely! And this wasn't the only amazing thing recently, this whole weekend was a God-thing. He really pulled out all the stops, and I'm so blown away and humbled at how good He is."

Before she could go on, a waiter came with the menus and they silently made their selections. Paul chose the mu shu pork, and Josie opted for moo goo gai pan. Both came with a choice of fried or steamed rice, and an egg roll, and Paul also ordered a plate of won tons.

They made small talk as they waited for their food – what do you do for a living, when did you start your business, are you from here, where did you move from – the usual getting-to-know-you dialogue. Paul told her he had come for college and stayed because Norris and Tuney were so good to work for. Josie was born and raised there. Their food arrived, and Paul didn't hesitate to bow his head and give thanks when the waiter had finished and walked away. Josie was very impressed.

After a little more small talk, Paul steered the conversation back around to the shop, and in particular, the Armor of God display. Josie told him how easy it had been to put together because she already had most of it, so when she saw the armor at the home décor store, it was like it was meant to be.

Chapter 8

Paul asked her with a straight face, "What do you call an overweight knight?"

Her brow furrowed as she thought about it, "I don't know, what?" Her fork was in mid-air, about to go in her mouth.

"Sir Cumference," was the answer, still poker-faced.

Everything on her fork fell to her plate as she laughed without restraint, and Paul was no longer able to keep up the dead pan, her laugh was too charming.

Josie said excitedly, "Are you practicing on me? Okay wait," she started fanning her face and took a few deliberate breaths. "I'm ready."

She was anything but ready as she stared steadily into his eyes. Paul cracked another corny joke and her mouth started twitching. At the second joke, her hand came up to cover her mouth, but it was obvious she was struggling behind it. After the third joke, she couldn't stand it anymore and laughed unreservedly.

Paul was laughing too, loving her reactions. Josie became aware first that they were staring at each other and dropped her eyes to regain composure.

Paul decided to ask what she meant about her amazing God-thing weekend, and Josie's face lit up like a thousand candles as she started to tell him about Chloe's decision to trust in the Lord. He

Talks To A Picture Of Jesus

watched as her expression turned to righteous anger when she talked about Van, then sorrowful as she tactfully talked about her hard childhood and feelings of unworthiness, leaving out anything that might be construed as gossip, then finally sheer joy as she described Chloe's salvation. At that moment, Paul had never seen anything more beautiful in his life, than the expression of ecstasy on Josie's face. He knew he had to see her again.

The lunch hour was winding down, so after a few minutes, he brought the conversation back around to the competition. "Would you like to go with me on Saturday, Josie? I would like it if you were there, cheering me on, but not making me laugh, so don't go 'Whoop, whoop, go Paul go!' or anything because I'd probably bust up if you did."

"Ha, ha, ha, ha! Oh, now I'm going to have to bring pom poms!" Pretending to do a cheer, she said "Paul, Paul, he's our man! If he can't do it, no one can!"

"Ha, ha, ha, ha, ha! Well I suppose if you just have to cheer for me, then who am I to stop you? So you'll go then?"

Josie had smiled and laughed so much during lunch that her cheeks were getting tired and sore. Nevertheless, she could not stop smiling if her life depended on it. She replied, "I would like that."

At that moment, Paul reached across the table for her hand. He looked deeply into her eyes

Chapter 8

and said, "Josie, I know we've only known each other for a very short time," Josie's eyes widened slightly and he continued, "but I feel like we have such a connection. It's like we've known each other forever. So it just feels perfectly natural to ask you this question. Josie Montgomery," Paul stopped there and paused for effect, enjoying the shocked look on her face. He slyly continued, "Can I have a bite of your moo goo gai pan?" He was rewarded with that beautiful unrestrained laughter once more.

Lunchtime had come to an end, so Paul paid the bill and they made their way out of the restaurant. It just so happened that Ernestina and Hector had just parked and were walking up at that moment.

"Josie!" said Ernestina, giving Josie a hug. "We were just talking about you and how talented you are. Linda is thrilled with her wedding dress, and you want to know what she did? She went and showed Benny! Ay, that girl! The husband isn't supposed to see the dress before the wedding, but at least she wasn't wearing it. But still, it's bad luck!"

Ernestina would probably have gone on and on, but Hector, being used to the way his wife rambles, took one of Josie's hands and didn't let his wife deter him from speaking his peace. "Josie," he said, "you have done something truly wonderful and amazing. You have made my mija the most beautiful

Talks To A Picture Of Jesus

bride ever, and I thank you, and I praise God for you and your ability. May you always use it to honor and glorify Him."

His sincere words touched Josie's heart. "Oh, thank you Hector. I'm so glad I could do this for Linda, and I'm glad you all like it, including Benny." She and Ernestina laughed as Ernestina rolled her eyes.

Hector turned to Paul and said, "This one here, she's special. She's a keeper."

Paul studied her for a brief moment, before responding, "Good to know."

The parents of the bride continued on into the restaurant and Paul walked Josie past his car and down to hers. "I have your work number, but can I have your cell? I'll call you and get your address so I can pick you up on Saturday like a proper date."

She got her phone out and said, "What's your number, I'll text you real quick." He gave it to her and pulled his phone out to look for her text. It came immediately, so he added her to his contacts, and took her picture before she could protest, so her picture was a part of the contact information.

"I had such a good time!"
"Me too!"
"I'm looking forward to Saturday."
"Me too!"
"Okay, I'll talk to you later then."

Chapter 8

He leaned in for another hug and Josie marveled at how right it felt.

"Bye."

"Bye."

Josie got into her car and Paul headed back to his car. Josie wanted to scream, but knew she couldn't just then, not while he was still a few feet away, so she tensed up and said "Aaahhh!" as quietly as she could. Paul got in his car, and let her pull out first. She headed North and he headed South. Paul pushed his Sync button and said "Call Mark." Soon, the phone was ringing and Mark was on the other end.

"Hey buddy, what's up?" Mark answered.

"Guess what, Mark, let me tell you about a God-incidence that just happened ………." Both were engrossed, one in her thoughts and one in his conversation, so neither one paid any attention to the new Matthew West song playing on K-Love®.

It's six a.m. and she's awake,
it's time to start her day.
A quick shower, makeup, and a curling iron,
some jelly and toast and she's on her way.

A good day's work, then it's five o'clock.
She thinks she'll stop at the gym.
A bite to eat, TV, then it's off to bed,
and sooner or later, it starts again.

Talks To A Picture Of Jesus

*She'd like to meet a nice guy,
and maybe start a family someday,
But she's not into the bar scene,
and no one in her church looks her way.*

*But she keeps the faith and doesn't regret the love
that never was.
Late at night, when all is quiet and still,
she talks to a picture of Jesus.
Yeah, she talks to a picture of Jesus.
It's six a.m. and he's awake,
he just signed in at the gym.
Some bench presses, sit-ups, and a curl or two,
a shower and shave and that's it for him.*

*A good day's work, then it's five o'clock
and he's already out the door.
It's bumper to bumper all the way home, before he
gets there he stops at the store.*

*He'd like to meet a nice girl,
and maybe start a family someday,
But he's not into the bar scene,
and no one in his church looks his way.*

*But he keeps the faith and doesn't regret the love
that never was.*

Chapter 8

Late at night, when all is quiet and still, he talks to a picture of Jesus.
Yeah, he talks to a picture of Jesus.

It's six a.m. and she's awake,
and he's already at the gym.
Well, they don't know it, but today's the day.
I'm going to do something special for them.

I've set things in motion and I've made a good plan,
and pretty soon they're going to see,
It's not going to be a coincidence,
'cause all along they've been talking to Me.
Talking to Me | Talking to Me | Talking to Me[viii].

𝒯𝐻𝐸 𝐸𝒩𝒟

Dear reader, although this is a work of fiction, God's love for you is not. Our sin separated us from God, and maybe like Chloe, you feel as if God is mad at you and could never forgive you. Nothing could be further from the truth. In an unbelievably astonishing act of love, He sent His son, Jesus Christ, to take our sin upon Himself, and Jesus said that anyone who puts their trust in Him would be saved. Saved from what? Saved from the day we all stand before God for judgment. None of us, even the seemingly best of us, are good enough to enter into a place so holy that no sin can exist – the very presence of God. But when we put our faith in Jesus, the Bible says *our unrighteousness* is exchanged for *His righteousness*. It's not a fair exchange, but that's the extent of His love!

Do you long for forgiveness? It's there for the asking. Do you feel an emptiness inside you and are searching for something to fill it? Nothing is more wonderful than to be filled with the peace of God. If you haven't put your faith in Jesus, won't you do it today? You can talk to Him right there where you are sitting, standing, lying down, or even kneeling. Whether you are at home, in a car, at work, or in an airplane, it doesn't matter. He will hear you, just talk to Him. Ask for forgiveness, put your faith in Him, don't put it off any longer, do it now! It's the best decision you'll ever make!

---

[i] K-Love® and Air1® are registered names of Educational Media Foundation
[ii] American Family Radio (AFR)® is a registered name of American Family Association
[iii] Family Life Radio (FLR)® is a trademark of Family Life Communications Inc.
[iv] (How Can It Be, 2016)
[v] (O Come to the Altar, 2015)
[vi] (Clean, 2015)
[vii] (Get Down, 1999)
[viii] (Morris, Gayla, Talks to a Picture of Jesus, not published *yet*)

Song Title: How Can It Be
Song ID: 4028199
Song Writers: Jason Ingram/Jeff Johnson/Paul Mabury

Open Hands Music (SESAC) / So Essential Tunes (SESAC) / Flychild Publishing (SESAC) / Ponies Riding Shotgun (ASCAP) / (admin at EssentialMusicPublishing.com). All rights reserved. Used by permission.

Song Title: O Come to the Altar
Song ID: 24
Song Writers: Mack Brock/Chris Brown/Steven Furtick/Wade Joye

Music by Elevation Worship Publishing (BMI) / (admin at EssentialMusicPublishing.com). All rights reserved. Used by permission.

Composition/Song Title: Clean
Writer Credits: Natalie Grant
Copyright: © 2015 SeeSeeBubba Songs (SESAC) (admin. by Music Services). All rights reserved.
Used by permission. International copyright secured.

Made in United States
Orlando, FL
11 December 2023